Penric's
MISSION

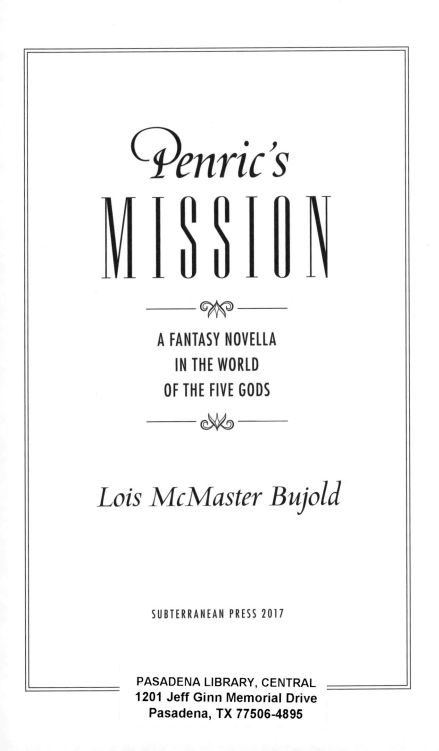

Penric's

MISSION

A FANTASY NOVELLA
IN THE WORLD
OF THE FIVE GODS

Lois McMaster Bujold

SUBTERRANEAN PRESS 2017

First Hardcover Edition

ISBN
978-1-59606-844-5

Subterranean Press
PO Box 190106
Burton, MI 48519

subterraneanpress.com

I

"**D**ESDEMONA!" PENRIC BREATHED, awed. "Will you look at that *light*."

He leaned on the railing of the Adriac cargo ship coasting slowly up the narrowing Gulf of Patos, and stared eyes-wide at the rocky shores of Cedonia. The dry clarity of the air made the distant granite mountains seem as sharp-cut as glassmaker's crystal. The angled sun of morning was the color of honey. He tilted back his head to take in the astonishing blue vault above, so deep it was dizzying; he felt he might dive up through it as into the sea, endlessly, and never drown.

It was what he imagined enchantment should be, in some myth or legend of personified elements,

The Man Who Fell in Love with the Sky. Mortals, he was reminded, did not usually come out well at the ends of those tales.

"Yes, but by noon it will scorch that pale scholar's skin of yours to blisters. Keep yourself covered. We'll have to see about getting you a proper hat," his demon returned, speaking through his mouth as prosaically as the bossy older sister he sometimes imagined her to be. But he thought she was not unmoved by the sight, shared through his eyes, of the light of the land of—could you call it her birth?—that she'd last departed, what, over a hundred years ago?

"Longer than that," she sighed.

He pressed his finger to his lips, warning her not to speak aloud in company, and moved around to the prow, keeping clear of the crewmen shifting ropes and sails. Half-a-dozen other passengers clustered there to catch a first glimpse of the city that lent the gulf its name. The ship came about and tacked toward the farther shore, climbing a slight headwind.

A tumbled slope drew aside like a stage curtain, revealing their goal. Spread across the wide amphitheater of the gulf's head, Patos seemed built of the bones of this land: stone houses with red tile roofs, stone streets, arched and colonnaded; the familiar five-fold shape, high on one hill, of a stone temple. A broad stone fortress guarded stone quays reaching out into the clear blue waters, where a dozen other cargo ships crowded, offloading.

The grove of cranes and masts made up for what seemed to Penric's eyes a decided lack of trees, which was in part why his ship's heavy lading of cut timber was expected to be welcomed trade. A bit slow, bulky, boring; a ship for ordinary men with ordinary purses to make passage in. Such as a lawyer's young clerk, carrying a sheaf of unsigned merchants' agreements and a hopeful marriage contract. All entirely bogus. He adjusted the strap on his shoulder and touched the leather case that held them, plus the second set of documents that was much less dull sewn covertly inside its lining.

Velka gave a little wave as Pen joined him on the forward deck. The man was a Cedonian mercantile agent with whom Penric had made friends, or at least friendly acquaintance, on what he had been assured was a remarkably smooth three-day sail from the Adriac city of Lodi, and on whom he'd been happy to practice his Cedonian. Smiling slightly, Velka said, "Still excited for your first trip to Cedonia?"

"Yes," Pen admitted, grinning back, still inebriated by the morning light and not even bothering to be sheepish. The young clerk should certainly be allowed such elation.

"I expect you will find it full of surprises."

"I expect so, too."

Des passed no comment, even internally, but Pen felt she watched the harbor scene as keenly as he did.

Two oarsmen in Cedonian Customs' tabards rowed a green-painted boat out from the quay and swung alongside Pen's ship. He picked up his single valise and followed Velka with the first batch of passengers to disembark, making his way over the side and down the rope net without mishap. When it had rid itself of its human freight, the ship would go on to another quay at the Imperial naval shipyard and arsenal to discharge its timber. Penric mused on the rationale, which rather escaped him, of one country selling essentials for shipbuilding to another country when they might, some future year, be at war or at least in chronic naval clashes with each other. Well, the puzzle did not fall within the ambit of this mission.

Imperial Customs consisted of a long wooden shed housing tables, a few agents in official tunics, some bored guards, and a dull air of bureaucracy. The passengers shuffled into line and turned out their goods for inspection. His clerk, when Pen took his turn, examined his fake papers and wrote down his fake name and age and fake business with only mild interest. His valise was dumped out on the table and his possessions pawed through, as the clerk looked for Pen knew-not-what.

His belongings had been carefully selected back in Adria to fit his travel persona, and included nothing of interest; most certainly not his white robes of a divine of the Bastard's Order, or the white, cream, and silver shoulder braids marking him as a Temple sorcerer. Nor even the four-cord green braids of a teaching physician of the Mother's Order, which had been foisted on him back home in Martensbridge even though he had declined to take oath to a second god. The faint ink stains on his long fingers might well have belonged to a lawyer's clerk.

In any case his most secret and dangerous contraband, his chaos demon who gave him his uncanny powers, passed entirely unsuspected.

Velka, lingering to speak with some port official, waved Penric on, and Pen emerged once more into a light grown even sharper. He stepped away briskly, not wanting to be lumbered with a companion at this stage. He wondered if he should first seek out the man he'd come all this way to bargain with, or go find lodgings. Perhaps locate the fellow, then pick lodgings convenient to him. Asking around the harbor marketplace for his quarry's address would leave a trail of witnesses to his interest. There must be something more discreet.

Good thinking, observed Desdemona. *Your best bets will be up by the provincial governor's palace, or some tavern near the army barracks where the soldiers gather.*

It felt strange to have a visceral sense of the layout of a city he'd never set foot in before, but one of Desdemona's previous riders had lived here for some years. Over a century ago, Pen reminded himself. Things would have changed, although probably not major buildings or streets, not with all this stone.

The marketplace, a semi-permanent little village of booths and awnings, smelled of fish, ropes, tar, and spices. Offerings included used clothing, domestic tinwork and ceramics, and food, exotic— to Pen—oranges and lemons, dried figs and nuts and strange bright vegetables, olives and their oils. The vendors and patrons showed nearly as much variety, men and women, and children of both sexes running about adding their notes of chaos. Clothing tended to loose linens, tunics and trousers for the men, demure draperies for the women. Skin colors ranged from almost Roknari bronze to olive to a deep brick tan on those who clearly worked outdoors.

Hair was as varied, curly to straight, sun-streaked bronze, dark copper, brown, but mostly black. He was glad he'd taken the advice to dye his own to an unassuming brown for the journey. His blond-white hair stood out even back home; here, where he found his mountain-average height suddenly half a head taller than most men around him, it would have blazed in this sun like a signal beacon. His eyes he could do nothing about, save to squint a trifle. He attempted to shrink in a clerk's stoop.

Completing his fascinated survey of the market, he began a stroll up a street leading toward the hill hosting the governor's palace. The noise of the harbor—seabirds crying, workmen and vendors shouting, the creak of the cranes, clack of hooves and rumbling of carts—at first eclipsed the steady double-time of booted feet coming up behind him.

When he turned, the squad of half-a-dozen soldiers was almost in his face.

"Halt, you!" cried their sergeant.

Penric tensed on his toes, but obeyed, blinking and smiling, free hand out empty and unthreatening. "Hello," he tried in a friendly tone. "Can I help you?" Only then did he see Velka running behind them, pointing at him.

"That's the spy! Arrest him!"

His first impulse, to try to talk himself out of this contretemps, died as he reflected that a more thorough search of his leather document case must surely find its hidden compartment, and the duke's secret letters, and then no amount of talking would help. But his well-filled purse was hung hidden on a cord around his neck, his case strap slung over his opposite shoulder, unsnatchable.

As the sergeant pulled his short sword from his sheath and swung it upward, Pen thought, *Des, speed us!*

From his point of view, his would-be assailants slowed. Pen flung his valise at the sergeant, knocking him backward, and ducked another man's leisurely sword thrust. His own movements always felt as though he were fighting through oil when he did this, but he drove force through his legs and turned, taking the first few steps of a sprint away. *Where*, he would have to work out later.

But *now*, he bounded directly into the other half of the squad who'd turned onto the street just above him, bearing down upon him with raised truncheons.

He evaded four languid blows as sinuously as any striking snake. Jerking successfully away from a fifth swing smashed the side of his head into a sixth, with a lot more power than even the man who wielded it had probably intended.

The world turned to stars and snow as he gasped and dropped, cracking his head on the stones *again* as his flailing hands missed catching himself. Nauseating black clouds bloomed in his vision as he did not, quite, pass out.

Passing out would have allowed him to evade the pain and misery that followed. Plenty of strong hands combined to hoist his long body up and hurry him back down the hill and through the gates of the shore fortress. Shadows flickered overhead, then stone. At first he thought he was swooning for certain as the world darkened, despite the continued drumming in his skull, but they were just going underground; an orange blur of torchlight wavered past him. The passage narrowed, widened, narrowed again. Widened again.

He was held down and efficiently stripped of case, boots, purse, belt and belt-knife, and his outer garments. Someone grabbed him by the hair and growled, "What is your real name?" Pen couldn't even groan in reply, though he panted and then, suddenly, vomited on his interrogator. As defenses or even revenges went, it seemed weak, but at least the man leapt back, swearing.

"Bosko, you hit him too cursed hard. He can't talk in *that* state."

"Sorry, Sergeant! But it was his fault—he ducked into me!"

"Never mind," said Velka's voice. "I daresay this will answer all the questions anyone has." Velka, yes, seemed to have taken loving possession of the leather case. A smile of satisfaction curled his lips. Pen grew sorry he hadn't let Des cheat the man at dice after all, shipboard.

"I don't suppose he can climb down the ladder on his own, now," said a soldier.

"We could just drop him in."

"Aye, if you want to break both his legs."

"So is he going to be needed for anything, later? Aside from his execution?" asked the sergeant of, Pen guessed, Velka.

"Too soon to know. Best preserve him for the moment."

A brief, professional debate among the soldiery resulted in Pen, dressed only in his shirt and trousers, being lowered into darkness by a rope wound painfully under his arms, shepherded by a soldier on a twisting rope ladder. His bare feet, then knees, then the rest of him found cold, raw rock as he collapsed. Rope, soldier and ladder all disappeared upward. The scrape of a heavy stone overhead cut off both the voices, and the last faint reflections of the torch. Utter silence. Utter darkness.

Utter aloneness.

Only...not for him.

"Des," he groaned. "Are you still with me?"

A shaken pause. "They'd have had to spatter your brains all over the street for me to be anywhere else."

Despite his current throbbing pain, his curiosity prompted him to ask, "Where would you have jumped?"

A sense of surly thought. "Velka."

All else being equal, a demon forced to jump by the death of its rider usually went to the strongest other person in the vicinity. "Really?"

"He would not have lived long." A pause. "And he would have died in all the lingering agony I could arrange."

Pen wondered if that was how a chaos demon said *I love you.*

More or less, Des said in their silent speech, as his lips grew harder to move. *Pen, pay attention. You mustn't swoon. Your skull is cracked and you're bleeding inside it. We can burn closed the blood vessel, but we have to open a hole to let out the clot before the pressure kills you.*

You want me to trepan myself?

I'll do it, but you have to stay conscious. I can't work it if you...if you...

Understood.

Destructive medicine. Sometimes, it saved lives. Sometimes it didn't...

His head was in so much pain already, exploding open a hole the size of his fingertip hardly made a difference. The spurt of blood seemed small, but a little of the numbness left his lips. *Yes, that's right,* and he wasn't sure which of them said it.

Can I pass out now? Hurts...

No. Stay awake. We have to finish shifting the clot.

That, too, was right. Familiar. And a very unpleasant prospect. Was Des in as much pain as he was? Maybe not, but if his mind and body broke down, she would fragment, too. *Can't be fun for you either.*

No.

After a little, he asked, *Des, can you still light my eyes?*

Yes...

In a moment, the blackness pulled back. With no light at all to work with the effect was peculiar, oddly colorless, but his sense of the space and the shapes around him grew secure. They seemed to be in a round chamber quarried out of the bedrock, about fourteen feet high and seven wide, its chiseled walls curving steadily inward to the small port at the top presently blocked by the heavy stone.

Penric studied the cruel angles, and meditated on the mountain-climbing experiences of his youth. *No. I don't think even I could scale this one.* And certainly not in this condition. In his imagination, on the trip over, he'd confidently posited that no locked door could hold them. *Is this place meant to be proof against sorcerers?* Had Velka penetrated *that* secret, as well as his others?

It's a standard Cedonian bottle dungeon. A place they put prisoners they want to forget, it's said.

Ever been in one before? And, unsaid, *Ever got out of one before?* Except the hard way, he supposed, minus her rider.

No.

In a little while, he crawled to the wall and clawed up far enough to turn and brace his shoulders against it. They paused to tease out the last of the clot, and he felt gingerly at the spreading wetness behind his ear, soaking his walnut-dyed queue. It wasn't going to add up to enough blood loss to kill him. At least, not on this side of his skull.

He sat up and concentrated on keeping breathing. As ambitions went, it seemed much reduced from this morning's, but it was challenge enough for now.

AN UNMEASURABLE time later he began to wonder how he had betrayed himself to Velka, how he had failed in discretion or simply in acting, not that he'd cast a hard role for himself. Try as he might, he couldn't remember. Velka hadn't been another sorcerer. Nor a shaman. Nor, certainly, a saint. He'd not used any uncanny means to flush out Pen's secrets.

For that matter, who was Velka really? The patriotic Cedonian merchant he seemed? Or an agent of another kind?

For what it's worth, said Des, *I can't see our mistake either.*

It was kind of her to try to make him feel less stupid, Pen thought. This, his first confidential diplomatic mission, had been supposed to be a simple one, and, if he brought it off ably, bore the promise from both duke and archdivine of more such opportunities for travels to new places. A bottle dungeon hadn't been on his imagined itinerary.

Some period after that, he began to wonder if he would die; then, as time ground formlessly on, just how he would die. Executed in some frightful manner? Or simply forgotten to death in the dark? Which wasn't the dark for him. Nor would he die alone; Des was a friend he couldn't outlive. He could grow reconciled to that, he guessed.

I should have liked to see that sky again, though.

It was a shamefully long time after *that* when he finally thought, *What will happen to the man I was supposed to meet?* The full cost of his failure began to sketch itself to his vivid and well-stocked imagination, and he cursed some dozens of histories he'd read that suggested exactly how, in gruesome detail. *Five gods. What will happen to General Arisaydia?* It wasn't just Pen who might pay for this fiasco with his life.

But not Des. That, at least.

And another small blessing: "No sun blisters, anyway!" He giggled. But his mouth was too dry, and then he choked.

Pen, said Des uneasily. *You're starting to fray, down here. If you can't hold yourself together, you won't be able to hold me. Hold!*

How? He laid his aching head upon his knees, reminded of why people trapped in unbearable pain sought death at their own hands.

Des said reluctantly at last, *Pray to your god. He's the only other one in here besides us.*

Pen considered this. For a long time. Then whispered, "Lord Bastard, Fifth and White," and faltered. He held up his hands in the black, fingers spread wide in supplication. "Master of all disasters out of season." Indeed. "I lay this day as an offering upon your altar. If it please you, take it from me."

That wasn't any of the prayers he'd been taught in seminary, almost a decade ago, but it felt right. And perhaps it was heard, for at length he slept.

᳇

A LONG time, it seemed to Penric, after he had been dropped into this hole, the stone scraped back, orange light flickered, and a covered pail was lowered on a hook. At the guard's shouted instructions, he rolled over and freed the hook, which rose upward as he could not. The cover was a crude round tray holding a small loaf of bread, only a day stale, a sticky block of dried fruit, mostly figs, and a pale square that Des assured him was pressed dried fish. He lifted the tray to reveal not a slops bucket, but a generous couple of gallons of fresh water and a wooden cup.

Pen drank greedily, then slowed, wondered how long it would need to last.

"I'd guess this to be a daily ration," Des opined. "Drink up anyway. You need it to heal."

He managed part of the bread and some shreds of the fruit, but after one bite couldn't face the fish, for all that Des urged it on him with the concern of an anxious mother, insisting it was common food, and strengthening. It smelled. And had bones in it, albeit as fine as stiff hairs. And, and *bits*.

So he was fed, watered, and left alone which, for the first three days, was all he wanted. The cell's diameter gave him room to stretch out fully on the floor, even as it made impossible the old mountain-eer's trick for shinnying up a crevice by bracing one's back and feet against opposite sides.

On the fourth day, he sat up and began to tend to his own wounds in more detail. Des could speed the healing of his abused skull and counteract infection, but it was definitely uphill magic, and she needed somewhere to dump the disorder. Normally there were enough minor vermin around to make this a trivial task, but once she'd eliminated the spiders and a few other shadowy things with far too many legs that rippled across the walls, others were slow to arrive. On the fifth day, they enjoyed a boon when a rat came up the central floor drain that doubled as Pen's slops bucket. Des fairly pounced on it. Pen was afraid he would then be trapped in this bottle with rotting rat reek, but Des, compelled to unusual frugality by their circumstances, not only creamed off the death but reduced the corpse to dust within an hour, and he used the dregs of his daily water to rinse it back down the drain.

For lack of other pastimes, he found himself crouching at this sink hoping for more rats like a winter fisherman back home beside his hole sawn in the lake ice. He missed a flask of warming spirits to keep him company, or friends to trade lies with, but at least there was Des. He studied the drain, which was no wider than his palm, drilled down through solid stone. Maybe he was not that desperate yet...

"Not ever," snorted Des. "Even you are not skinny enough to fit down that pipe. And it only goes to a borehole scarcely bigger."

"Empties into the sea, I expect." The smells and occasional drafts that came from it were more estuarial than cloacal. But no, probably not the drain. Widening a passageway through it by chaos magic could be a month's tedious labor, as lengthy and tiring a process as tunneling with the spoon that he did not have. Up was another unfavorable option. He could work apart the arch around the port, at some risk of dropping large stones on his head and making guard-attracting noises, but levitating up there would still be impossible. Waiting to be hauled up out of the dungeon for interrogation by his captors still seemed his best and easiest chance at escape, certainly until his fractures mended. He was perilously hot with their healing, masking the chill of any incipient prison fever.

He shouted questions upward during the daily visit from his keepers to swap out his rations pail, but they were never answered.

Three rats later, his skull, though still tender, had stopped aching in a way that made him want to cut his own head off. He dutifully managed to choke down the disgusting fish and not gag it up after. Des beguiled some time by telling him stories from her many past lives with her former riders, all women, or rather, ten women, a lioness, and a wild mare. The mare had been the point at which the demon first escaped into the world from the Bastard's hell, or repository of chaos, or whatever it was. There had been many theological arguments back at seminary as to the exact nature of the place, which Pen thought Des should be able to settle as she was the only one who'd been there, but she'd claimed to have no memory of it because its very disorder did not allow memory to form. All her personality—personalities—was, or were, something she had acquired afterward, imprinted on her by the endurance of matter.

Her tales were good, but in this lightless, sound-less place, began to take on a hallucinatory quality. He'd usually experienced them as words, if inside his own head, and an impression of animated gestures like a storyteller in a marketplace. Now he began to see flickering pictures. It was much like those disturbing nights when he dreamed not his own dreams, but hers.

The more disturbing as it became harder and harder to tell day from night in here, or dreams from waking.

II

***T**HE SHADOWS IN* the municipal magistrates' court-and-prison at midnight made Nikys want to crawl inside her own skin. She drew her dark green cloak closer about her and padded as silently as she could after the jailer she'd bribed to let her in to see her brother. This jailer would do more—or rather, see even less—if she could bring her plan about.

He led her up stone stairs and out onto the third-floor gallery overlooking the courtyard. In the night silence the boards creaking under their feet seemed screams, not mouse-squeaks. No dank dungeon cells with iron bars on this level, just a row of small rooms that could as well have been civic offices, apart from their heavy locked doors with narrow, iron-bound slots.

Nikys tried to extract the political meaning from this choice of confinement: more austere than house arrest; not so vile as, say, those oubliettes down at the old harbor fortress. Maybe it was mere prudence. If they'd attempted to arrest and hold the young general out at the army barracks or in the shore fortress, he'd likely have been smuggled aid before this. For all that he'd commanded in Patos for barely half a year, he was already starting to grow popular with his men, if only for his diligence in getting them paid on time.

Although on the lately disputed southwestern borders, men had followed him for much less. *Victory is the best pay an officer can give his men*, Adelis had once remarked. *And vice versa.*

A brilliant campaign of maneuver and strike, it was said, turning back the Rusillyn incursion with half-forces, wits, and spit. (Adelis himself had called it the Bastard's Own Dysentery.) In any just world, in any other *country*, his labors should have resulted in promotion and reward. Not semi-exile to a minor provincial post, and heightened political suspicion. Doubtless exacerbated by his mother's blood ties to the Imperial House, for all that several prior too-successful army generals had ridden on the shoulders of their soldiers to Cedonian imperial power without such bonds. But if Adelis had such ambitions, she'd never seen a hint, and she'd known him from the day of their births.

The jailer peered through the door slot. He did not startle the night by knocking, but just called softly, "General Arisaydia? You have a visitor." Handing Nikys the shaded dark-lantern, he unlocked the door and let her slip within, but stayed nervously on guard outside.

Adelis, dressed only in a loose shirt and string-tied trousers, sat on his cot, blinking in the sudden spear of light. As Nikys set the lantern on a little table and swept back her hood, he swung out bare feet and bolted upright to embrace her, the power of his grip silent witness to his anxiety. She embraced him just as hard, then pushed away to search his face, hands, arms for signs of torture. Bruises, yes...but no worse than he might have picked up at sword practice.

As his wits caught up with the rest of him, he shoved her back, though not loosening his drowning-man's clutch on her shoulders. "What are you doing in here at this hour?" he said through his teeth. "Or at all? Five gods, Nikys! I prayed you'd have the sense to stay clear of all this!"

"*All this* came to me. The day you were arrested, the governor sent men to search my house. They took all my letters from you, and my old letters from Kymis, what could they want with *those* I was so furious—"

His jaw tightened. "Did they hurt you?"

She shook her head. "Just shoved me back when I protested."

Despite it all, the corners of his lips twitched. "Did you hurt them?"

"Gods witness I tried," she sighed. "They knocked down my servants, ransacked the house. Tore up floorboards and pried apart paneling and furniture, especially in your chamber. Turned out all the clothes chests and left everything in piles. Although they were clearly after, oh, I don't know what they were after, but they didn't really pillage us, and no one was raped. A lot of small valuables turned up missing after they left, but you'd expect that." She drew breath. "Adelis, where did this all come from? All I could find out is that you are accused of plotting treason with Adria, which is nonsense."

He shook his head. "I swear I don't know. They said they'd seized my correspondence with the Duke of Adria, detained his agent, but I'd never made any contacts with Adria. They didn't let me see the evidence—said it had gone in a courier pouch to Thasalon days before, and this arrest order was the result. Not that they need be authentic letters for this sort of move."

"Forgeries to entrap you, do you think?"

"Maybe."

She flung up a hand. "Later. We can talk later. Dress, gather your things. I have to get you out of here, right now."

"What?" Instead of obeying, he stepped back and stared. "Nikys, is this some sort of hare-brained rescue scheme?"

"Yes," she snapped, declining to waste time arguing about the embedded insult. "Hurry!"

Instead, he shook his head. "Bad idea."

"Staying here is a worse one."

"I agree it's not good, but nothing would convict me in my accusers' eyes—in the emperor's eyes—faster than fleeing like a guilty thief."

"Do you imagine they haven't convicted you already?"

"There has been no trial, no hearing."

"When did *you* grow so naive?"

He smiled sadly. "If I didn't run from four thousand screaming Rusillyn tribesmen, I'm not going to run from this."

"They attacked from the front. This is an ambush from behind, in the dark."

"Oh, the Rusylli did that, too."

She grimaced, fierce in her frustration. "What in the world is your plan, then?"

"Stand my ground. Argue my case. Continue to speak the truth."

"And if that ground has already been cut from under you?"

"I did not commit treason, and I will not. I am not without friends, as well as enemies, at court."

"Argue your case from a safer place!"

"There isn't a safer place, not within the bounds of the empire. And to leave it would turn the false charge true."

She leaned her forehead against his shoulder, so frenzied she nearly bit his shirt. "Adelis. It has to be tonight. I can't do this again. I spent all I had on the bribes just to get this far, and the horses. Suborned men don't give *refunds*."

He sank down on his cot and did a good simulation of a boulder, stolid and immobile. Stubborn.

It ran in the family. If she'd brought four men, whacked him over the head, and carried him out in a sack, she might have been able to do this. But when that look grew on his face, nothing less would shift him. She'd sometimes admired the trait, but not when it was aimed at her.

"You have to leave," he argued in turn, "and stay well away. You're bound to be watched, but you're not enough threat to anyone in your own right for them to go after you without provocation. For the love of all the gods and goddesses, for the love of *me*, don't give that provocation."

"You're saying I should do nothing, just freeze to the ground like a hare menaced by a hawk?"

"That would be a good start, yes." He swiped his hands through his dark disheveled hair, clenched them on his knees. "*Please* don't try to engage with something so far over your head as this. The last thing I need is for my enemies to realize how effective a lever on me you could be."

Tears were leaking down her cheeks, and she hated their wet helplessness. "Curse all men, and their pride, and their greed, and their envy, and their *idiocy*." *And their fear.*

He grinned at her, his rich brown eyes crinkling. "Ah, that's my Nikys."

She couldn't scream here. She couldn't even *yell.* Another ten minutes of ferocious undervoiced argument moved him no further. He should have been made a siege commander, she thought.

Only the frightened jailer stopped it. He cracked the door and hissed, "That's enough. Madame Khatai, you must come away *now.* I can't stay out here any longer."

Adelis pushed, the jailer pulled, and she found herself once more on the gallery, bewildered in the dark.

He led her back down the stairs. Out the side archway to the entry with the postern door.

Where they found a troop of six guardsmen and a senior captain waiting for them.

The jailer had not revealed her; he whimpered, too, as they were roughly seized. Another lantern was unveiled and raised, pushing back the shadows.

"Where is he?" asked one of the guardsmen, sounding confused.

The captain stepped forward. Cornered, she yanked back her hood and raised her chin. Protests and subterfuge and lies jammed up in her mouth, choked by fear. *Wait. Give nothing away.*

"Madame Khatai." The captain grimaced. "Imagine meeting you here at this hour."

Oddly, his ironic tone steadied her. This was a man who would talk, not strike. Or at least talk before he struck. "If anyone here had possessed the common courtesy or holy mercy to let me see my own brother in the daytime, I would have. I took what I could get."

His glance seared the shrinking jailer. "So it seems."

"You mustn't blame him. I cried at him, you know." Which was true, if incomplete. The captain, she suspected, was not a man whom feminine tears would soften. But let him think this was just an anxious visit from kin, not an escape attempt, and perhaps the poor man would get off more lightly.

"And where is your brother?"

"Right where you people put him. Unjustly." Her lips drew back in something that was hardly a smile. "He claims the Father of Winter will support him in his innocence."

The captain vented a faint snort, but stepped aside to murmur to two of his men, who departed at a run. They returned in a few minutes to report, "The general is still locked in, sir."

The captain stared at her in some frustration. Had he hoped to catch her in the act? He said, conversationally, "We have your horses and your servant, you know. Rather a lot of baggage for an evening jaunt through town, don't you think?"

It wasn't as though she'd left them waiting at the prison's front gate. So, she'd been spied upon— make that, more *effectively* spied upon—than even she had suspected. Not that anyone who'd really known the general and his widowed sister could have been too surprised at this turn of events, but how many people in Patos was that, really? She lived retired by choice, and seldom taxed Adelis at camp; he in turn was respectful of her privacy.

Betrayed from before the beginning, it seemed.

Her dead silence was apparently not the reaction for which the captain had rehearsed, so he gave up trying to draw her out, replacing his heavy irony with sternness.

"Your efforts on your brother's behalf are understandable, Madame, but pointless. If you return here at midday tomorrow, the general will be given back to you freely, without impediment. In fact..."

He narrowed his eyes at her. "In fact, we will escort you home now, and guard your rest. And escort you back tomorrow. Just to make sure of it." He added after a moment, "We will, however, be keeping the horses."

"He is to be released?" The soaring thrill his words engendered died in her chest. That Adelis was innocent—or, be frank, something like innocent—she had no doubt. But he might mean only that her brother was slated to be summarily executed, yet have, as a pious mercy, his body returned to his family, such as she was, for burial instead of being hung on a gibbet outside the city gates as a lesson to other would-be traitors. Whatever the answer, the captain already *knew*. And the pity in his face frightened her far more than the sternness.

He didn't reply, but just surrounded her with his men and marched her out into the winding streets of Patos.

So, they'd both been right, she and Adelis. Her pathetic escape scheme was doomed to failure. And his remaining in his captivity was a horrible, horrible mistake.

AT NOON the next day the soldiers came once more for her, as threatened, and escorted her in reverse back to the same side entrance of the municipal prison.

The captain swept through, saw them, and grimaced. "You're too early. Keep her here. You three, come with me." And to Nikys, "Wait."

So they waited, shifting from foot to foot. No one spoke to her—nor to each other, no small talk or barracks chaff or crude complaint. They offered her neither insult nor reassurance. The unnatural silence stretched. Her head throbbed, as if it held too much blood, as if she'd been hung upside down.

One of the soldiers returned leading a saddled horse—one of her own hiring that she'd thought lost last night. He joined the wait, as wordless as the horse, which blew through its nostrils and cocked a hip.

The stillness was abruptly shattered by the most inhuman scream Nikys had ever heard. Even muddled by intervening walls, it rose high and piercing, then broke, then rose again. Then cut off sharp, as if the raw throat from which it reverberated had clenched closed, or been sliced through. The horse tossed its head and sidled uneasily.

It couldn't have been Adelis's voice...could it? Even at age ten when he'd broken an arm falling off his pony, he'd vented no more than an odd little *Eh!* Perhaps it was only some thief, convicted for a fifth time and paying a hand in penalty? Such punishments were sometimes administered here, she thought. *Please, please, let it be some thief...*

The remaining soldiers had stopped looking at her, or around, or at each other. To a man, they stared at the ground. Afraid? Who wouldn't be, after hearing that unholy sound? She was terrified, her body shuddering as if in the winter wind, though sweat dampened her all over.

No. Stranger than that, she realized. *They stand ashamed.*

At length, silhouettes appeared in the bright archway to the inner court, two men supporting a third stumbling between them. *Adelis?* Not a corpse on a litter, to be sure, but relief didn't wash through her. The solid form was familiar, its constricted posture not. His body was hunched, lurching, as though he were overtaken with wine-sickness.

It was only as they came near that she saw the pale bandage wrapped around his head, and realized why they were now willing to release the genius general to no more stern a warder than his sister.

Oh gods oh gods oh gods oh gods oh gods…
They've put out his eyes.

III

---

*P*ENRIC GUESSED IT might have been ten days when the stone was dragged back and not replaced, but no hooked rope dropped to collect his empty pail. Instead, a few feet of a leather hose were pushed over the edge of the hole, though not far enough to be anywhere near in reach. The guards were silent shadows in the wavering torchlight, its wan glow grown as brilliant as the sun's in Pen's staring, dark-adapted eyes.

"Now what?" he called up, not expecting a reply.

"Mercy for you, madman," someone growled back down.

"I'm not mad." *Rather angry by now, though.*

"You babble to yourself all the time."

"I'm not talking to *myself.*" *Just to the voices in my head. All ten of them.* Not, he knew from long experience, a useful thing to mention.

A snort, and the—pair?—of sandaled feet shuffled away.

A few minutes later, the hose bulged, coughed, and began to disgorge a steady stream of what Pen hoped was water. He tested it by thrusting a hand in the flow. Yes, seawater, not, say, rainwater or sewage. Odd...

"Are they giving our little home a washing and flushing? It certainly needs one."

His throat constricted strangely as Des replied, "No. That's not it."

The water was coming in faster than the drain was leaking it away. Had they blocked the far end of the borehole? Pen splashed his bare feet uncertainly in the growing puddle.

Des continued, "They mean to drown us in our cell. Like a mouse trapped in a bucket. A means of disposing of a prisoner without leaving a mark on his body."

Why should they care about that? And... "Don't they know we can swim?"

"For how long?"

"Hours? Days?"

"They have days."

"If they have days, they could just stop feeding us, and wait." This suggested…what? *Something has changed, out there.*

After a few minutes, when the water topped his ankles, Pen said in aggravation, "They never even questioned me." That had remained his primary hope of escape—let him only be lifted out of this stone bottle, and whatever bindings or tortures or hulking guards were offered, he'd have been through them and gone from this fortress like an egg through a hen. Although he'd planned to endure through the first few questions, to gain some idea of the shape of his situation. "It's going to take a lot of water to fill this cell."

"They have the whole sea as a reservoir."

The fortress was above sea level, although only just, and so was the cell, or high tide would have come up twice a day to flush his wastepipe. The hose-water flowed steadily, not in spurts like a ship's bilge pump. It was draining from some pre-filled tank, perhaps, not being lifted on the spot by men with muscles, or animal power. His mind darted down a tangent, calculating by his hard-won geometry the volume of the cell and the probable rate of flow from above. *Thank you, Learned Lurenz,* and he never thought he'd remember the sharp tap of that rod on his woolgathering young head with gratitude. "Six hours, maybe? Eight?"

"They won't fill it to the top, just to over your head. Pen, attend! Should I burst the hose?"

That would certainly delay things, although one of those things seemed to be 'the inevitable.' About to assent, he paused.

It was only parlor-magic. When he'd first moved over the mountains a year ago—along with six mule-loads of books and two of clothing—to take up his duties with a new archdivine, he'd found the heat of Adria's humid coastal plains oppressive. Lighting fires with a muted spark was the first destructive magic he'd ever learned, and the easiest. Running the process backward was a much subtler challenge. But with practice, and some thinning out of the vermin in the archdivine's palace in Lodi, he'd devised a trick for pulling water out of the air into a large hailstone, to drop in his tepid drinks. Prudently, he'd not shown off his novel skill, not wanting to be pressed into work as a magical ice machine for the pleasure of his superior's many highborn guests.

It hadn't kept the archdivine's cousin the duke from purloining him anyway, when he'd wanted a secret envoy with a reputation for cleverness and a native's command of the Cedonian language to effect...a disaster, it seemed.

Don't think about that now. You haven't time.

Had that been Des, or himself? In any case, yes, he did have time. Several hours of it, he guessed.

"How soon do you think they'll be back to check the cell for drowned mice?"

"No idea."

If they expected him to flounder in immediate panic, maybe not that long? No controlling that. He leaned his shoulders against the cell's curving wall and composed himself in patience, forming his plan.

Your plan is to freeze us to death before we can drown? Des asked plaintively.

His lips curled up for the first time in days. "Have you never watched the mountain raftmen in the spring, breaking the winter-cut logs loose from the river ice for their journey downstream?" Both Ruchia, his demon's immediate prior rider, and Helvia before her had been cantons-born just like Penric. "It's like a dance."

"A dance with death! …Have you ever *done* that?"

"A few springs, in my youth, I helped the local men in the valley of the Greenwell." Pen reflected on the memory. "Didn't tell my mother, though."

Hah. She added grimly after a while, as the water lapped his knees, "This is going to be costly."

"Yes. But consider the alternative."

As the seawater reached his thighs, he wondered aloud, "Do you suppose they know I am a sorcerer?"

Des hesitated. "It's not sure proof, but I'd think if they did, there would be a goat or a sheep or some such tethered at the top."

His head cocked back in momentary mystification, but then the answer slotted in. *Oh.* "To contain you safely after you jumped, till they could decide how to dispose of you?"

"It's an old trick when executing a sorcerer, yes."

"You wouldn't like that."

"No. So kindly stay alive, Penric."

When the water reached his shoulders, he commenced, starting a thin sheet of ice in the center of the cell. Hand to the wall and pushing, he walked slowly around the perimeter, to keep the water moving and his tiny ice floe centered. His body grew warm with the working of his magic, welcome this time since the Cedonian seawater, while tolerable by Penric's standards, was still much cooler than a man's blood, and had been leaching his strength away in increments. Hunger and thirst, too, would start to sap him if he let this drag out.

And Desdemona was growing...he was never sure what to name it. More excitable, perhaps, in these early stages. They were still a long way from the uncontrollable mania that overtook her when they tried to work too much uphill magic too fast, but it seemed discourteous to stress her beyond need.

Also dangerous.

Des muttered an obscene agreement, sign of sorts. "But you realize," she said in sudden cheer, as he plowed through water past his chest, "with this skill, you need never die of thirst in a desert."

Pen coughed a seawater-laced laugh. "Not my most pressing concern, here, Des..."

His ice disk grew thicker, descending downward in the middle; he tried to keep the top surface relatively flat. He needed to generate rather more than his own body weight, he guessed. As the water reached his chin, he clambered aboard.

And *up...*

The hose end was just beyond his reaching fingers. His bare feet on his floe were chilling, and, worse, melting potholes. He attempted a jump, missed, slipped, and ended up splashing into the water, barking his elbow painfully on the wall and being pinched against it by the pitching ice-brick. Brine in his eyes and nose stung, the taste bitter and metallic in his mouth. He came up spitting and heaved himself atop his float once more.

This time, he waited a little, letting the floe and himself settle as much as they could under the ongoing spout of water from above. Tested his balance more carefully. Gauged. Stretched. Coiled. And *UP...*

One hand closed around the slippery leather, then the next. The jet of water in his face cut off as his hanging weight pulled the hose closed over the edge of the port. One hand over the other, *don't let go, don't fall back...* He flopped an arm over the keystone circle. Then he was out altogether, collapsing across the dungeon's paved floor. He lay gasping for a moment.

Rolling over, he peered one last time down into the watery, deadly well. "You realize," he wheezed, "that once that ice melts"—which it was already starting to do, and swiftly—"they're going to have *no idea* what we just did."

Desdemona borrowed his mouth for a black laugh that echoed very demonically indeed. He clapped his hand across it, but grinned back.

He was still sprawled wet, barefoot, brimming with hot unshed chaos on the prison floor of a guarded fortress. Alone, on the edge of an unknown country. No idea if it was day or night outside. *Not the time to plan a triumphal celebration yet, I don't think.*

Three bottle dungeons lay in a row in this close corridor, the other two thankfully unoccupied, so how special a prisoner had he been? A locked door at one end led, probably, to a guard post. The lock would be easy, the guards perhaps not. He followed the leather hose back the other way to where it issued partway up the wall from a small window, its normal barring unbolted and set aside for the occasion.

"Can we get out this?"

"Maybe. Better chance than the drain. Seems to run about two feet through the wall and open into a window well. I can't sense what's beyond that."

Pen leaned backward, reached through, turned his head sideways, and fitted himself in. A great deal of undignified wriggling later, and he was able to sit up in the outer well without actually snapping his spine. His long legs nearly trapped him, but at the cost of some contusions he managed to extract them without having to break bones. He stood up in the well.

He'd reached a sort of porch overlooking the sea. The stone tank rose nearby, a silent bilge pump standing near; unmanned at this hour, which was night *five gods be thanked*. He'd feared the sudden sunlight might have blinded him as effectively as the black below.

Something scuttled along the edge of the porch, and then exploded with a pop.

He'd not seen a rat do *that* before. *Quieter, Des!*

Hurts, she complained. *Also, how many times have I sat in the latrine with* you *sick when—*

Even after a decade, she could still make him blush. *Howsoever. How do we get out of this place?*

Your job now.

The obvious way out was to slip over the wall, swim quietly around to the harbor in the dark, and creep up over one of the jetties.

They stared down at the black, lapping sea with equal disfavor.

"No help for it," said Des at last, "unless you want to go back to the bottle dungeon. Carry on."

Penric sighed and climbed down into the foam-laced waters.

⟨❧⟩

AN HOUR later, salt-crusted and footsore, Penric sat in a stone laundry trough that drained a modest marble fountain, sited in a square fronting a middle-sized temple. He'd drunk his fill of blessedly clean water, and now faced the next task. He tried not to think about the several harbor rats and a luckless sleepy seagull they'd sacrificed in their wake down at the shore; Des, calmer, seemed back to visiting chaos only on less theologically questionable insects. One couldn't call it necromancy, exactly...

Lie back, said Des, in her practical Ruchia-voice, *and I'll get rid of your hair dye.*

"Really?"

They'll be looking for a brown-haired escapee. Also, your blond roots are growing out. It will be easier to lift the stain altogether than to try to work it around to match.

He decided to take her word, and besides, the fresh water was something very like a bath. He would have preferred to burn his prison-reeking shirt and trousers, but until he could replace them, this impromptu laundering would have to do.

So it was, after almost falling asleep in the trough, that he sloshed up and squeezed out his hair, letting it fall down his back—the ribbon for his queue was long lost. Not much time left till first light and people about, he gauged. He left a trail of wet footprints to the shadowed temple portico. Opening a simple lock was so routine by now that he didn't even pause in swinging the tall door ajar and slipping within. After that, it was rather like going shopping in the marketplace. In reverse.

The layout within was similar to home, with altar niches spaced around the walls and a central plinth for the holy fire, banked to coals for the night. Timber-built temples in the cantons boasted fine woodcarvings; here, the plastered stone walls were graced with frescos, their subjects ambiguous in the shadows, and mosaic tiles enlivened the floor. This was a neighborhood temple, he judged, serving the folk in the immediate vicinity, not so large or so well-guarded as the main provincial temple atop some higher hill. Nor so wealthy, alas. He found the Bastard's niche, perfunctorily signed himself, and checked the altar table for offerings. Swept bare for the night, unfortunately.

But this was the sort of prudent place that featured locked offering boxes in each niche. He flipped this one open and peered within. If it, too, had been emptied for the night...

A scant scattering of coins and other oddments lay within. His long fingers rapidly picked out the coins and left the less identifiable prayers, such as a coil of hair.

He contemplated his meager take. "The white god must not be much loved here. Or much feared."

"You wouldn't accept any of my suggestions for targets through town."

"Stealing from the poor is inefficient, and stealing from the rich is dangerous. Anyway, this isn't stealing. It's just...collecting my pay more directly than usual."

Des snickered. "I didn't think the Cedonian and Adriac Temples practiced such reciprocity."

"Same god." He'd known from the beginning that he served his god first, and the Temple second.

So far, he'd not found them often in conflict, and prayed it would stay that way.

Slowly, he circled the chamber. His hand hovered over the box at the Mother of Summer's altar, but then passed on. While he'd no doubt She would not begrudge a loan to her second Son's divine, Pen had refused Her his oath back in Martensbridge; it felt, if nothing else, rude to ask for Her aid now. He'd abandoned service to the Son of Autumn years ago, and the Daughter of Spring had never been his goddess. He finally stopped before the Father's altar.

"Pen," said Des uneasily. "*Nobody* steals from the god of justice."

"Borrows," he corrected. "I expect my collateral is good here. Maybe Locator Oswyl would vouch for me." He smiled to remember his friend back in Easthome, the most earnest devotee of the Father of Winter he'd ever encountered. He flipped open the box and raised his brows. "Goodness me."

"Somebody must be anxious for their lawsuit," Des suggested.

"Possibly both sides. Though trying to *bribe* the god of justice seems missing the point." Or he supposed some poor—evidently not-so-poor—call it *distraught* man might be praying for a child, or for ease for a dying father. He signed himself and bowed his head in any case. *I shall try to use it well, Sir.*

He doubled back to collect the cloth from the Bastard's altar to carry it all in, relocked all the boxes, and slid out again to the portico, closing the door quietly. Sky and sea were growing a strange clear gray. He could hear the clop of a donkey and creak of a cart, and, from open windows roseate with lamplight, people stirring and pots rattling.

Find a used-clothing vendor, find a cheap inn, find a breakfast that did not include dried fish; after that...

After that all this was going to grow harder. It wasn't a happy thought.

⟡

PENRIC QUARTERED the streets of Patos near the army barracks and parade ground, trying to puzzle out his approach. Walking up to the front gate and knocking seemed a poor one. In his new retrospect, it struck him how thin his preparation for this emissary's task had been.

He wondered if he'd been missed from the bottle dungeon yet. Fortunately, he'd found a clothing stall and food from a street vendor before being confronted by his cot in his little inn, for he'd fallen like a tree into the linen-covered, wool-stuffed mattress, and slept in profound exhaustion. When he'd woken in the late afternoon, he'd found he'd not lost as much time as he'd imagined. Unlike home, where people seized the afternoon to get as much done as possible before the dark and the cold closed in, here the citizens evaded the bright hours, crawling into the burrows of their houses to escape the heat and emerging just about now.

He wriggled his feet in his odd leather sandals. His workman's garb was unexceptional, a sleeveless tunic and trousers that were expected to ride short in the legs anyway. He'd knotted his hair on his nape, still blond but not hanging out like a signal flag. A countryman's straw hat shaded his eyes. His accent, broadly archaic from the far northern mountains of Cedonia, marked him as not from around here, so legitimately lost, without making him alien.

Until you start talking at length, and that scholar's vocabulary begins falling out, commented Des. *In that country accent, it's like a donkey opening its mouth and spouting poetry.*

I'll try to be more brief, Pen sighed.

Curse it, he had to start *somewhere.* He spotted a lone soldier, not an officer, leaving the squared-off barracks grounds, and angled over to accost him before he disappeared into the close, winding streets of the civil side.

"Pardon me. Can you tell me where to find General Arisaydia? I was given"—*Bastard's tears, don't say* a letter—"a package of figs to deliver to him."

The soldier stopped and stared. "Hadn't you heard? He was arrested. Four days ago, by the governor's guards. By Imperial order, it's claimed. I don't know where they took him, but he's sure not *here.*" He jerked his thumb over his shoulder at the military quarter now suddenly not Pen's goal.

Pen swallowed in shock. Seven or so days after his own arrest—if the two were connected, why the delay? Gathering other evidence?

"On what charge?" Pen managed.

The soldier shrugged. "Treason, I guess. They can slap that on anything. Sounds like shit to me." He hesitated, as if wanting to call back his unguarded words. "But what do *I* know?" He shouldered away from Penric and strode on, surly. Disturbed.

Seven days. Time for a speedy courier to ride to the Imperial capital, a day or two for debate, persuasion—plotting—a couple of days for an arrest order from high enough up to be returned? Very high up, it sounded like. Officers at Arisaydia's level could be moved around like game pieces only by the most powerful of hands.

However it had come about, it was plain that rumors were running through the army like dye through wool. If Pen wanted answers without bringing attention to himself by asking questions, he needed to find a place where the military talked to each other. Handily, several taverns catering to the soldiers' trade clustered in the nearby streets. He glanced into a few until he found one that was more crowded, and where his countryman's dress would blend in, and slipped inside.

He held a tankard of vilely sour ale and wandered about, listening for key words and especially for the key name. He found it at a table with half-a-dozen low-grade officers, a couple captains-of-hundreds and their lieutenants. He slid onto a stool by the wall and pulled the brim of his hat a little farther down over his eyes, and simulated a workman's tired doze. Well, simulated the doze; the tired was authentic.

"It was never peculation, not him," one scoffed.

"I'd not heard that one," said another. "Plotting betrayal with the Duke of Orbas, I was told. Or the Duke of Adria. Or of Trigonie. Some frigging foreign duke or another, anyway."

Universal scowls greeted this claim.

"Or no duke at all," growled a grizzled captain. "Some trumped-up charge by those eunuchs at court, more likely."

Another made a crude joke at the expense of mutilated men, which his comrades seemed to find more black than funny.

"Yes, but what's Arisaydia *have* that that crowd of mincing bureaucrats would want to steal?"

The grizzled captain shrugged. "The loyalty of the Army of the West, for starters. Enough highborn bureaucrats, whether they still have their balls or not, have military nephews who might like to filch a rank they can't bloody earn."

"Surely the emperor," began another, but his captain held up a stemming hand. He began again more carefully, "Surely those Thasalon *courtiers* are not to be trusted…"

Men at this level could hardly know more than Penric did, but their talk was alarming.

No, sighed Des. *All standard army-issue bitching about the civil government, so far. It doesn't seem to have changed in a hundred years.*

Huh.

The talk had turned to other complaints when a new man joined them, and Pen had to keep himself from sitting bolt upright. He was a younger fellow, broad and brawny, and had the sunburned brick-colored skin of most of the men here, but his face was strained and ghastly, drained to a sallow tinge. Wide-eyed and breathless, he fell into a seat on the bench, where his comrades obligingly shifted to give him room, and said, "Five gods, give me a drink." Not waiting, he seized one from a comrade, who yielded it up with a surprised eyebrow-lift. "I just heard—" He tipped back the tankard, and his mouth worked, but he couldn't seem to swallow. He had to struggle for a moment before he could choke it down.

"Arisaydia," he gasped out. "Yesterday noon in secret at the municipal prison. Imperial order."

"Released?" said a man hopefully, then faltered.

"Executed?" growled the grizzled captain, voice grim as iron.

The new man shook his head. "They blinded him with boiling vinegar."

Shocked silence. Bitten lips.

Pen bent on his stool and swallowed back vomit.

Don't you dare, said Des. *Don't give a sign.*

"Princely," observed the gray captain, in a weird sardonic lilt that might be rage, or grief, or swallowed curses. "Thought us army mules usually got hot irons through our eyes."

"Not an honor I'd care for," muttered another.

The other captain leaned back and sighed. "Well, that's done him. What a gods-forsaken waste."

"Is he still in the prison?"

The new man shook his head. "No. They gave him over to his twin sister, what's-her-name, I heard."

So what is *her name...?!*

The men were easing back as they took this in, scowling but not, apparently, moved to leap up and start a military mutiny at the news this afternoon. Someone secured the messenger his own tankard, and he gulped deep. Some moved their food aside, but kept their clutches on their drinks.

"Hope she's a good nurse," said a lieutenant.

"Or will help him to a good knife," said another. "Either one."

Pen panted in horror, so, so grateful for the straw hat, its brim now down to his chin.

"Are they really twins?"

"Who knows? Story I heard was that *he* was the son of old General Arisaydia's highborn wife, and *she* was the daughter of his concubine, whelped on the same day. Unless the midwife swapped them in secret, to give the old man an heir."

"That's an old rumor."

"Funny, you never heard it around till he was promoted so high, so young..."

"Well, he's a poor blind bastard now. Whether his parents were married or not."

The mood of the table blighted, the party broke up, most men finishing their meals and drifting out, a couple settling in for deeper drinking. Penric, as soon as he could stand without shaking, made his way into the street, now half-shaded in the angled, descending sun, and found a wall to prop his shoulders against.

Gods, Des, now what?

Start back to Adria, I suppose. Not through the port of Patos, by preference.

Acid bile burned Pen's throat at the thought of such an empty-handed retreat. No, far worse than empty-handed.

It made no sense. The Duke of Adria had fancied to hire the demoted and presumably disaffected general as a mercenary captain for his own endemic and inconclusive wars against his neighbor Carpagamo. The private letter he'd received from Arisaydia himself had suggested it, and the duke had taken him up on it...

Taken the bait?

But it wasn't *treason*, no more than Penric exchanging his service across the borders from the new princess-archdivine of Martensbridge to the archdivine of Adria. The duke hadn't planned to use Arisaydia against Cedonia, after all. It was just...a little delicate.

It shouldn't have been much worse than that, unless, unless, what?

There had to be a hidden half to this somewhere that Pen was not seeing. As he'd not seen how that Cedonian, Velka, could have guessed Pen's real mission. Unless, of course, he'd already known...

But, Bastard's tears and Mother's blood, *blinding*. He'd seen burns and bone-deep scalds when drafted into his apprenticing-and-more at the Mother's

Hospice in Martensbridge. Up close, in some bad cases. He didn't have to *imagine* anything.

"I have to do something about this."

Five gods, Pen, what? The damage is done. It's time to cut our losses and fly.

"I don't know yet." And then, in the next three breaths, he did.

He would need particulars on the sister, her name and domicile, and then a better used-clothing merchant. A better bathhouse, too, that offered services of a barber and a manicurist. An apothecary. A knife-maker's shop serving some very specialized needs. And more. How providential was it that the Father of Winter had filled his purse...?

It was going to be a busy night. He pushed off from the wall. "Let's go find out."

IV

NIKYS SAT IN the garden of her rented villa and tried to eat…breakfast, she supposed it must be, this being morning. A morning. Which?

It had been, what, two days?—since she'd brought Adelis back here, clinging to his saddle, his labored breathing as frightening as weeping. Half her servants had fled after the visitation from the governor's men and not returned, so, to her loathing, she'd had to employ the soldiers who'd escorted them to support him stumbling to his upstairs bedchamber and lay him down. She hadn't wanted them *touching* him. She'd ejected them from her domain as swiftly as she could thereafter, without thanks, but a provincial guardsman still lurked outside her front door, and another beyond her back wall.

After that, the nightmare had commenced. She'd sponged her brother's body, dressed him in clean linen, coaxed him to eat, with poor luck, forced him to drink. He'd not cooperated much. She'd seen Adelis in a dozen bad moods in the past, exhausted or frustrated or enraged, though generally with the army or the Imperial court rather than with her. She'd never before seen him *broken*.

It was lovely in the garden in this first light. Water trickled musically through clever stone channels from the tiny spring that had made the villa, though old, such a wonderful find, half a year ago when Adelis had invited her to join him at his new posting. On the pergola that shaded her little table and chairs, grapevines shot forth leaves that seemed to expand by the hour, with green sprigs of new grapes peeping shyly through them. Bees bumbled among the flowers. On the far end, where the kitchen garden grew apace, dew sparkled off a spiderweb like a necklace of jewels carelessly dropped by some passing sprite. The space breathed charm, grace, ease, surcease from troubles.

This morning, its lying beauty *offended* her.

She ate the other half of her boiled egg, with a bite of bread to force it down, and a swallow of cold tea to force down the bread. When she finished, she'd have to return to Adelis's bedchamber and try again with the bandages stuck to his face. He'd screamed when she touched them, and struck out—blindly, of course, and so he'd connected at his full strength in a way he'd not done since they were squabbling children. His full strength had been much less, then. She rubbed at the deep bruise on her cheek, and buried her face in her hands.

She couldn't weep. Or sleep. Or eat. Or breathe...

Control yourself anyway. You have to go back now.

When she looked up, an apparition sat across from her.

She was so bewildered she didn't even jump, though her jaw fell open as she stared.

Her first thought was not *man*, or *woman*, but *ethereal*. Luminous eyes as blue as the sea in summer. Hair an astonishing electrum color, drawn back in a knot at the nape but with a few strands messily escaping to catch a sunbeam in a wispy halo. And nothing human should have skin so milk-pale.

She dismissed her furious fancies. It was most certainly a man. Her gaze skipped down the long, folded body. Wiry arms, hands too large and strong for a woman, nails cut blunt and scrupulously clean. Sandaled feet too long to be feminine, chest too flat, hips *much* too narrow. Drawn back to the face, she discovered an inexplicably cheery smile and white, sound teeth.

He wore an undyed sleeveless tunic to his knees, belted at the thin waist, with a sleeveless jacket in dark green over it, suggesting, without quite being, the garment of an acolyte of the Mother's Order.

In a soft, friendly tone, her hallucination spoke: "Madame Khatai, I trust?"

She swallowed and located her voice, sharp-edged with alarm: "How did you get in here? There are guards." Less to keep people from going in and out, she suspected, than to mark and report who did so.

"Perhaps they went off-duty? I didn't see any."

"My servants should have stopped you."

"I'm afraid I didn't see any of them, either," he said as if in apology.

That she could believe, she thought grimly.

"Pardon me for startling you," he went on in that same soft voice.

Stunning me.

"—my name is Master Penric. I am a physician."

She rolled back in her chair. "*Apprentice* Penric, I might believe. You can't be a day over twenty-one. Less."

"I'm thirty, I assure you, lady."

He claimed an age the same as hers, and she was a century old, this morning. "I might grant twenty-five."

He waved an airy hand. "Twenty-five it shall be, then, if you prefer."

"And *Master...*?"

"In all but final oath." His smile grew rueful.

"Hnh."

"My credentials aside, some of your brother's officers took up a collection to hire me to attend upon him. For reasons you may understand better than I, they strongly wished to stay anonymous." He raised his blond brows, and she grimaced, unable to gainsay the likelihood. "But my fee is paid, and here I am."

"For how long?"

He shrugged. "As long as I'm needed." He gestured at the large case by his feet. "I brought supplies, and a change of clothing." After a moment he conceded, "I might not have been anyone's first pick as a physician. But I was the one who would come. ...And I'm fairly good with burns."

That last did not so much decide as dismast her, setting her adrift on dangerous shoals of hope. Her gaze caught on those scrubbed, thin-fingered hands. She might believe those hands, though she was none too sure of his tongue. She had no trust in this sudden stranger, she had no trust in anyone, but she was so benighted *tired...*

Perhaps he read her surrender in her posture, for he continued, "I should examine the general as soon as possible. I'm so sorry I couldn't be here earlier."

"Follow me, then." She pushed herself up, frugally drained the dregs of her tea, and led him into the house. "But he's not a general anymore, you know." She had come to hate the very sound of the betraying—betrayed—military title, which her brother had so cherished.

"What should I call him, then?"

"Arisaydia. I suppose." She did not invite this Penric fellow to *Adelis.*

As he lugged his case up the stairs after her, he asked, "Has he spoken much?"

"A little."

"What has he said?"

She stopped before Adelis's door and scowled up at the physician. "*Please let me die.*"

He hesitated, then said quietly, "I see."

As she opened the door he took a very deep breath and squared his shoulders—she revised his age downward again—and followed her inside.

Adelis lay as she'd left him to go down to breakfast. Nikys glanced at the scullion she'd set to watch him. "Any changes?"

The boy ducked his head. "No, lady."

"You may go back to the kitchen."

The blond physician held up a hand. "When you get there, boil a pot of water and set it to cool. And then another. We're going to need a lot."

"The water left from my tea should be cool by now," Nikys offered tentatively.

"Good. Bring that first." Master Penric nodded, and the boy retreated, staring back curiously over his shoulder.

Nikys went to the bedside and took Adelis's hand. Its tension told her that he did not sleep. "Adelis. I've brought you a physician, Master Penric." The man had brought himself, more like, but she doubted Adelis would respond well to that news, either.

Below the cloth wound around his face, still not unwrapped from that first awful day, his lips moved, and he growled, "Go away. Don't want him."

Nikys perforce ignored this. Her hand hovered over the grubby makeshift bandage. "I'm sure this should come off, but it's glued itself to his skin. My maid said it should be ripped off, but I didn't let her."

Adelis spasmed on his bed, one fist wavering up; Nikys dodged it. "Is that cack-handed hag back? Get rid of her!"

"Shh, shh. She's gone. I won't let her in here again, promise."

"Better not." He subsided.

Penric, coming to the bed's other side, let his hand pass over the cloth and cleared his throat. "In the woman's defense, there is a treatment, debridement, for the reduction of burn scarring that involves…something like that, which she might have seen sometime and misunderstood. Not for this, though." His voice went tart. "If the fool woman had done that here, it would have torn off his eyelids."

Both Nikys and Penric clapped their hands over their mouths, she to keep her breakfast down, he as if to call back the blunt words. Adelis jerked and groaned. Penric grimaced in weird irritation, and added hurriedly, "Sorry. Sorry!" casting Nikys an apologetic head-duck. "Burns are a gruesome business, I can't deny. I hate them."

A faint snort from the bed.

Penric eyed the heavy supine figure under the sheet. "What have you given him, so far?"

"I obtained some syrup of poppies. I'm almost out, though." Adelis loathed the opiate, but he'd accepted it from her hands this time. She didn't think it had quelled the pain enough for him to sleep, but it had kept him too quiescent to fight her, lying in sodden silence. Too quiescent to rise and seek to do himself harm?

"I brought a good quantity. He can be given some more before I start."

The physician cleared space on the wash table, opened his case, laid out a cloth, and positioned supplies upon it in a precise, organized manner that subtly reassured her. He began by measuring out his syrup into a little vessel with a spout; then he held up Adelis's head and tipped it into his mouth, stroking his throat with a finger as he swallowed it down. His movements were gentle, but firm and sure, practiced-seeming. Mindful, but not in the least hesitant.

The scullion returned with the first of the water, and Penric laid a towel under Adelis's head and commenced dribbling it over the blindfold. "This will take some time to loosen," he remarked, "but it won't be difficult. And I promise all his skin will stay on."

A fainter snort.

It seemed an optimistic prediction, but Nikys longed to believe it, so said nothing. As she sat in her chair, watching the man watching her brother, her head nodded, and she jerked it back up. As much to keep herself awake as for any real curiosity, she asked, "Are you from the northern peninsula? Your speech is a little odd."

He hesitated, then smiled again. "My mother was. My father was a Weald-man, from the country over the *other* mountains, to your far south and east."

"I've seen men like you in the emperor's guard in Thasalon. They were supposed to be from islands in the frozen southern sea. Fierce warriors, I was told, but ill-behaved visitors." Well, not just like him, as he didn't look the least like a warrior. But some of the big brutes had been similar in coloration, if not so, so...so much so.

"I'm a well-behaved visitor, I assure you."

"Where did you study medicine?"

"...Rosehall. It's in the Weald."

Her brows rose. "I've heard of it! A great university, yes?" Despite her reservations, she grew more hopeful.

He looked at her in surprise. "I didn't think Cedonians knew much about my father's land."

"I've lived in the capital, and seaports. People get around. Like you."

His smile grew a bit strained. "Yes, I suppose so."

At length, done fiddling with water and oils, he took sharp scissors from his case and cut through the cloth on either side of Adelis's face. He undid the wrap from around the back of his patient's head and dropped it out of the way, resettling him on the towel. Adelis groaned in fear. "You need not watch this," Penric said over his shoulder to Nikys.

"I'll stay."

"Hold his hands, then."

She went to the bed's other side. "To console him?"

A long finger flicked out and tapped her purpled cheek. "So he can't hit me."

She half-smiled and did so; Adelis gripped her spasmodically back.

Penric took a breath, closed his hands on either side of the stiff cloth, and lifted it delicately. The vile mask seemed to puff away from Adelis's face like a dry leaf, pulling...nothing at all.

She swallowed hard at the destruction that was revealed.

Blisters, huge puffs of membrane-thin skin bulging with liquid, ranged over Adelis's upper face and *quivered*. His eyelids were a horror, rising out of his eye sockets like round bladders. What was not white and swollen was violently red and pink. As Nikys recoiled, sickened, Penric leaned forward, staring fiercely into what had been her brother's eyes as if he were trying to see right through his skull. But he said only, "Huh."

He caught Adelis's hands on their way to feel his own face and yanked them down hard, the first ungentle gesture she'd seen him make. "No. No touching. Stay on your back. That skin is barely stronger than a soap bubble, and we want to preserve those blisters intact for as long as possible. They're protecting you, little though it may feel like it."

Adelis panted, but obeyed.

The physician's brilliant blue eyes seemed filled with jostling thoughts, but Nikys couldn't begin to guess what they might be. "I think what I most need now, Madame Khatai, is for you to go get some real rest. I'll stay here and keep watch. Come back and relieve me at nightfall." He beamed sunnily at her.

"I'll bring you both food, later. Or have it brought."

"That would be excellent." He hummed, as if mulling something, then said, "If I'm going to be living in your household for a few days, we'd best give some thought how I am to be explained to your other servants. I'd suggest you tell them you've hired me on to be your brother's male attendant. Which is not actually untrue, among its other benefits."

While she couldn't imagine why anyone, even the politically hostile, could object to Adelis being seen by a physician however oddly he'd been delivered to them, she was reminded that among her erstwhile servants was one certain spy. She nodded slowly. "All right."

She went out to make preparations in the kitchen, and see to the arrangement of the small spare bedchamber. She didn't think she could sleep, but when she reached her own room on the other side of the atrium and sat down on her bed, she felt as if the weight of an oxcart, complete with ox, had been lifted from her shoulders.

She was still crying from the sheer relief of it when she fell asleep.

SHE RETURNED as instructed at sunset. When she eased open the door, Master Penric leaped up holding a finger to his lips and reeled out of the room. He clutched her hands and shook them up and down like a long-lost relative. His palms were feverish. His wide grin at her was nearly lunatic.

"He's asleep, miraculously. When he wakes up, get more water down him. Don't let him touch his face. I'll be back in a while and measure out the next dose of poppy syrup."

And then she wondered if he'd been drinking, or maybe sampling the poppy juice himself, for he called over his shoulder as he bounded down the stairs, " 'Scuse me, but I havetogokillsomerats now."

"What?"

"Mice? Mice would be all right, but you need more of 'em." His voice faded as he dodged not to the front door, but out the back way. "Has to be something useless lurking around this neighborhood. Stray dog would do a treat right now. Sweet lord god Bastard, deliver us *something...*"

She blinked, closed her mouth, shook her head, and went within. Sitting and watching the slow rise and fall of her brother's chest beneath his sheets as the shadows deepened, she decided she didn't *care* how strange the blond man was, if he could get Adelis to sleep like that.

V

*P*ENRIC GAUGED HIS distance in the dark from the neighbor's roof to the garden wall, leapt lightly, and settled himself down atop it for some composing meditation. The sleepy provincial guards, it appeared, had been instructed to attend to the villa's entrance and the postern gate in the rear wall, and that was just what they were doing. The one at the back had curled himself up against his assigned door and was currently napping, combining two tasks.

A bat fluttered by against the stars, but Pen let this one go, since his body had finally cooled. This neighborhood outside the city walls had lacked the swarm of big, aggressive rats like the harbor's, but he wasn't going back down *there* tonight. Des had left a trail of destruction through all the small vermin within her range, but with this much chaos to divest, insects had scarcely repaid even the moment's attention they took. Private middens had yielded more red-blooded prey, including a few slinking suburban rats, and what he thought might have been some kind of hedgehog. Pen regretted the mangy, worm-riddled street cat, but they'd been desperately hot and at least the poor beast no longer suffered.

"Eyes," muttered Pen. "They're so small. Why should this engender so much more chaos than making several times my weight in ice?"

His demon couldn't wheeze, exactly, so maybe it was just him as Des replied, "It may be the most subtle uphill magic you've yet attempted. The ice was big but simple. This mad healing you've thrown us into is *complex*."

Penric's initial plan, more selfish than charitable, had been simply to assure Arisaydia would survive his blinding, to evade the burden of yet another unwanted death in the pack Pen carried. It was only when he'd examined the man with all of Des's perceptions focused to their greatest intensity that he'd realized that the *backs* of his eyes, in all their impossible delicacy, were undamaged. And, suddenly, the hopeless had become merely the very, very tricky.

His first task had been the finicky release of beginning adhesions as Arisaydia's injured eyelids tried to grow themselves onto his steam-lashed eye-balls; then, rapid reduction of the ocular swelling, his skills and refined belladonna tincture working together. Pen had poured all the uphill magic he could into Arisaydia's own body's powers to heal, but that was a narrow channel that could only accept so much help at a time before it burst in a destructive back-blow. It was like trying to relieve a man dying of thirst using a teaspoon, but at least he'd kept the sips coming all the long day.

Arisaydia's survival was no longer in question, perhaps never had been. Pen had discovered the man in the bed to be above middle height, muscular and fit, obviously healthy before this catastrophe had struck him down. His face and arms and legs were that attractive reddish-brick tan common to the men of this region, though the parts of his body routinely covered by clothes more matched his sister's lighter, indoor version. His aquiline features, rough-cut in granite, were in her echoed in fine round marble; both shared the same midnight-black hair, his cut short, hers drawn back from her face and curling over her shoulders. Pen wondered what color his eyes had been. He could ask Madame Khatai, but it might distress her.

Speaking of which… "Do try to be more sensitive around the sister, Des. She's quite upset already."

Des snorted. *You have more than enough sensitivity for us all. To excess, as I have pointed out before.*

Bloody-minded chaos demon, Pen thought back.

The impression of an amused purr. *I do sometimes wonder how you ever survived, Pen, before you were us.*

Whereas I more often wonder how I am to survive after…

He stared down into the shadows beneath the pergola, where he had first seen and studied Madame Khatai from just about this vantage at dawn. She'd borne something of her brother's air of sturdy health, after a delightfully plump female fashion, but Pen didn't think he'd ever seen a woman's posture so expressive of utter despair. *I imagine she'd be quite pretty if she smiled.*

Des's response was sardonic: *So what is she when she isn't smiling?*

Penric contemplated the conundrum. "Heart-breaking. I think."

Was Des taken aback? *Oh, Pen, no. This isn't the time or place for one of your futile infatuations. This isn't a place we should be in at all. We should be making our way back to Adria.*

"...I know." Pen sighed. He pictured the man in the upstairs bedchamber whose life his fumbled packet of papers had somehow destroyed. No—he eyed the pergola—two lives, it seemed.

You hardly destroyed Arisaydia all by yourself. You had some expert help.

Aye to that. The increasing suspicion that he'd been *used* was a growing itch in Penric's mind. But by whom, and where, in this tangle of events? "Who around here would know who Arisaydia's enemies are?" He answered his own question before Des, this time: "Arisaydia would. For a start. If I could get him talking instead of just groaning." And, he was now sure, not *if* but *when* he did, who might a man trust more than his physician?

Des's silence would be tight-lipped, if she'd had lips. After a while she remarked, *I know you have no*

Temple orders for this. And I've felt no god move. You have embarked on this entirely on your own, Pen. How great a step from independent to renegade?

Or how many little slippery ones, more probably. And Des could not, would not, stop him, though she wasn't beyond making him stop to think. "Shall I pray to my god for guidance, then?"

They both fell silent, considering the fifth god each in their own way.

What would you do if you got it, and it wasn't what you wanted to hear?

"…Maybe I'll wait for Him to call on me."

Des shuddered. *I suppose you think that is an* amusing *joke.*

Pen's lips stretched in something almost a real smile as he dropped over the wall.

VI

OVER THE NEXT few days, Nikys's household settled into a strange, limping new routine. Their safety was balanced on the knife's edge, she knew, of the continued inattention of the provincial governor and whatever cabal in the capital—and she could probably guess the most likely men—who had engineered Adelis's downfall. They were doubtless waiting out there for the word of his death, from the shock or infection or despair. She was disinclined to give them the *satisfaction*. Although she supposed a long, silent convalescence followed by a retreat into some hermitage, religious or secular, would serve their purposes just as well. From here forward, Adelis would carry his imprisonment with him, at no further cost to the empire.

She'd made no move to replace the servants who had prudently scattered after the arrest; she wondered how soon the ones who'd lingered would realize how little coin she had left to pay them, and follow. Well, not the maid, the gardener-porter, and the scullion, who'd come with the villa rather like the furnishings, and would stay after the current tenants decamped. Which would be when? Adelis had paid her rent through the half-year, but the end of that term was coming up in a few weeks. Possibly why their landlord had not moved to evict his politically poisonous lodgers already.

Not that any woman could scheme how to hold household when she had *absolutely no idea* what her resources were going to be. Still, Nikys could make some shrewd guesses. Adelis's army pay would be cut off, of course, and all the property he'd inherited from his mother and their father attainted. Would the Thasalon imperial bureaucracy snap up every bit, or leave him some pittance? Would the small remains of her own dower and the military pension from Kymis be seized as well? That would be like a hawk, having taken a fat hare, returning for a mouse.

Their entire lack of visitors told its own tale. Some of his old officer cadre in the Western Army might have had the courage to come, but Adelis had been most cannily separated from them, now, hadn't he? Although given that some of his new men had sent that extraordinary (if extraordinarily odd) physician, she must hoist her opinion of them back up.

She and Master Penric had quickly found their way to a division of labor in the sickroom. The physician had taken a pallet on the floor, attendant-fashion, and guarded Adelis at night. Nikys relieved him twice a day: in the afternoon, when he rested in the garden or went out to discreetly restock his medical supplies, and in the evening after supper, when he departed on errands he never explained, though they seemed urgent to him. She'd almost swear she'd once encountered him coming back in through Adelis's *window*, which made no sense at all, so she'd dismissed the impression from her burdened mind. She wondered what other professional duties the man was leaving undone, to linger so diligently in this stricken villa.

The cook being numbered among the deserters, and the housemaid having proved as clumsy in the kitchen as she was in the sickroom, Nikys took over that task, not least because she trusted no one else with the preparation of invalid fare. Five gods knew she'd had plenty of practice cooking such for Kymis during that last miserable year. She finally managed to draw the physician to a midday meal with her under the pergola, hoping to quiz him frankly on Adelis's progress out of Adelis's earshot.

After they delivered the platters and jugs, she dismissed the scullion and sat herself down with a tired sigh, staring dully at her own plate feeling as if she'd forgotten how to eat. Master Penric poured her wine-and-water, and offered the beaker along with a smile fit to compete with the sunlight spangling his hair.

While she was still mustering her first question, he said, "I noticed your green cloak on the wall peg in the atrium, Madame Khatai. Is yours a recent bereavement?" He appeared poised to offer condolences, if so.

Dark green for a widow, yes, though she owed no other allegiance to the Mother of Summer. Sadly. "Not very recent. Kymis died four years ago." As his look of inquiry did not diminish, she went on: "He was a comrade of my brother's—something of an older mentor to him, when he was a young officer. Adelis felt he owed him much."

His blond brows pinched. "Were you payment?"

Her lips quirked. "Perhaps, a little. Our mothers were widowed by then, in reduced circumstances, so helping me to an honorable marriage to a good man whom he trusted seemed the right thing to do. Ten years ago...we were all younger, in a terrible hurry to get on with our lives. I wish I could have..." She faltered. But talking to this mild, pretty man seemed curiously easy, and he *was* a physician. His claim of *in all but final oath* seemed borne out, so far. "I wish I could have given Kymis children. I still don't know if it was some, some subtle physical impediment, his or mine, or just that he was called too much away to the border incursions. Adelis moved the world to get him back to me when he was wounded and maimed, as if I could somehow repair what the war had destroyed. But all I tried to do to save his life only prolonged his death. He cursed me, toward the end. I thought he had a point, but I didn't know *how* to let go."

It was the most honest thing she'd said about Kymis's dreadful last year to anyone—it was certainly nothing she could ever confess to Adelis—but Penric merely nodded, and said, "Yes."

Just *Yes*. Just that. It was nothing to burst into tears at the table about. She swallowed, hard. And awkwardly returned, "I suppose, as a physician"—in training, anyway—"you've seen the like. How it is to try and fail to keep some valued thing alive."

The flicker in his light eyes might have been from the movement of the dappled shade; he smoothly converted his flinch into a shrug, and she cursed her tongue, or her brain, or the day. Or her life. The smile he reaffixed was so like his usual ones, she began to wonder about their validity as well. But he said, answering her fears and not her words, and how did he *know*, "Adelis will live. I expect to get him up walking later today. He may not thank me at first, mind you."

Nikys gasped. "Truly?"

"Truly. He's a sturdy man; I think he'd have got that far on his own. If not, perhaps, quite so soon."

That far as compared to what? But he continued, gesturing with his fork, "So eat, Madame." He followed his own advice, munching with evident relish. For all his spare frame, he had an excellent appetite, of the sort that suggested starving student days were not long behind him. "You have a good cook. Shame to waste her art."

Nikys was about to protest that she was the cook, then realized Almost-Master Penric had certainly observed this. She smiled a little despite everything, and copied his example. After a few bites and a swallow of watered wine, she said, "That was what Adelis brought me to Patos for. To try to help me to a second marriage with another officer, if older and richer this time. I was happy to be here, but I hadn't the heart to tell him his efforts were a waste, that I would never again marry a military man. When we were talking last night, he apologized, the idiot. He seemed to think if he'd wedded me away to the protection of another, I would have been out from under all"—she waved a hand about—"this. Never mind the feelings of the poor hypothetical husband, to find himself suddenly kin to an accused traitor. Or what if he'd refused to admit Adelis to his household, when I brought him back blinded? I couldn't suggest that to Adelis, but it felt like how he describes ducking a crossbow bolt—you don't even know what you've escaped till it's over."

Penric scratched his head and smiled. "I quite see that. You *do*?"

"What?"

He coughed. "Nothing."

She grew graver. "I hate all this madness. But I can't help thinking about what it might have been like for Adelis if there had been *no* one loyal to him here, in this extremity." Would his tormentors have just cast him blinded into the street? The like had happened to other traitors. "I'm frightened all the time, yet I can't wish myself elsewhere."

"Frightened?" His brows flicked up. "Surely the worst is done, over."

It was her turn to shrug, mute with the weight of her dread. "Dying is easy. Surviving is hard. I learned that with Kymis." And no wonder she'd been thinking about her late husband so much these past few days, like a healed scar broken open again. "What will we do in the *after?*"

"That…" Penric sank back, sobered. "That is actually a very good question, Madame Khatai." And, mumbled under his breath: "About time somebody asked that one, Pen." He shook his head as if to clear it, and went on, "I am reminded. If Arisaydia is to be up and moving about, I want to devise some sort of protective mask for his upper face that we can easily take on and off. Line the back with gauze that I can soak with healing ointment, or change out and keep dry and clean, as needed."

"I think I might have something that would do. I'll look for it and bring it to you."

He nodded.

Somehow, while they were talking, she had emptied her plate. She drained the last of her beaker and studied the young physician. Abruptly, she decided he deserved to be warned. "I suspect there is a spy in my household."

He choked on his wine, coughed, mopped his lips. "Oh?" he squeaked, then finally cleared his throat and dropped his voice to its normal timbre. "What makes you say that?"

"The night before Adelis was blinded, I had devised an escape. I had mounts and a groom secreted near the prison. It was all for nothing, because Adelis refused to come with me. Which was also for nothing, as it proved, but anyway, my horses and servant were taken even before I left Adelis's cell, and soldiers were waiting in ambush for us at the entrance. They didn't even bother to arrest me. But someone had known my arrangements, and passed the news along, and it wasn't the jailer I'd bribed. I've not seen the groom since, so it could have been him, or any of the other servants who fled. Or it could have been one who stayed. I don't know."

"I see. How very uncomfortable for you."

"It's maddening, but it seemed the least of my worries at first." She frowned at him. "I don't know if any of this could follow you home, Master Penric. Perhaps, like me, you are too small a mouse for their appetites. But I should not wish to see you suffer for helping us. So, I don't know…be discreet?"

"I did know what I was getting into before I came," he pointed out kindly. "More or less."

"But still."

He waved a conceding hand. "As you say, still. I will undertake to be a very demure mouse."

She stared at him, thinking, *There's a hopeless plan*. But at least she'd tried.

VII

ARISAYDIA WASN'T EASY to coax out of bed. Penric fancied the man knew it was the first slippery step in undertaking to stay alive, instead of holding on to his imagined—begged-for—death like a starving child clutching food. But his dizziness, once he was upright, was no worse than anyone abed for a week might experience, and as he inhaled and straightened, it was plain that his body's native strength had been little impaired by his ordeal. He was still in pain, but Pen had found himself able to reduce the opiates more quickly than he'd anticipated, Arisaydia's slurred and muzzy mumbling giving way to crisper speech. Even if it was mostly swearing, so far.

Pen guided him out to the second-floor gallery circling the dual atriums, front and central, that admitted so much light and air into the villa, unlike the tightly boarded houses of the far-off mountain cantons. Did they ever get snow in this country? Arisaydia's hand trailed along the walls; Pen took the balcony side. Pen was almost sure the man wouldn't lunge for the rail and over, trying to finish the job that his enemies had started. Almost. It would make a dreadful mess on the mosaic floor of his sister's nice house, for one thing; for another, so short a drop was uncertain of outcome. So they strolled along arm-in-arm, like two friends out for a postprandial airing.

To distract Arisaydia from his surliness, Penric essayed, "Is it true that you and your sister are twins?"

It worked; Arisaydia's lips puffed in almost-a-laugh. "It was something of a joke among our mothers and us, when we grew old enough to realize we were unusual. If a woman could give birth to children of two different fathers on the same day, no one would hesitate to dub them twins. Why not the same for two mothers and one father?"

They came to a corner where the wall fell away; Arisaydia's free hand hesitated, clenched, then fell firmly controlled to his side. Only his slightly tighter grip on Pen's arm, as quickly reduced, betrayed his refusal to show whatever fear he must feel.

"A wife and a concubine are often bitter rivals in a man's house, but our mothers always seemed more like comrades-in-arms to us. Our father was flanked and outnumbered, but at least he had the wit to surrender. After he died, they continued to share their household—goods and grief and tasks portioned out all the same."

I wonder if they shared a bed, too? Des put in brightly. Pen set his teeth to be sure *that* didn't slip out, and asked instead, "Were they close in age, or by blood, or some such ties?"

"Not at all. Nikys's mother was twenty years younger than mine. My mother and father had evidently tried for children for years with no luck—it was long after he died that my mother ever mentioned her miscarriages in my hearing. So a child to share was certainly hoped for. And then, by whatever joke of the gods, there were two at once. We never knew whether to blame the Mother or the Bastard." Another turn brought a wall back within reach; Arisaydia barely traced it this time.

Nikys came out into the central atrium, holding something in her hand. She looked up at the sound of their voices. Her lips parted, a thrill illuminating her features as she saw them walking. Pen had guessed right; she was very pretty when she smiled. He felt a queer flutter in his stomach, to know that his work had put such a look on her face. And a following clench, to consider what she might look like to learn the whole story of Pen's involvement with her brother's woes. He heard the sound of her quick slippers on the stairs as he guided Arisaydia back into his bedchamber once more.

As he helped his not-very-patient patient sit up in bed, notably straighter than heretofore, Pen studied his face. The blisters were much reduced, shrunken and wrinkling; those that had broken were healing cleanly from the edges inward. The rims of his eyelids were silvery-damp—tear ducts, gods, how many rats had died for those tear ducts to open and work once more? Pen was still in grave doubt about the delicate irises. And nothing was more likely than for the brutalized lenses to go to cataracts, trading one form of blindness for another. Pen had heard of a horrifying operation tried in Darthaca, of cutting out clouded lenses and replacing their function with glass spectacles, but he hadn't heard that the success rate was high, and Bastard's tears, how could a person lie down and let someone take a knife to their eyes? Then he wondered how they'd held Arisaydia down for the boiling vinegar, and then he tried to stop thinking.

Arisaydia's lids were still too swollen to open, but it wouldn't be long now. Soon, Penric would find out what he'd done. More to the point, so would Arisaydia. Penric had not one guess how the man would respond. Except, probably not mildly.

Nikys entered, holding out her hand. "I wondered if this would do? It was an old masquerade mask. The beak should come off readily. Adelis went as a raven. For the battlefield, he said, which I thought at the time was morbid." She reflected. "Or a sly dig from the army at the bureaucrats. If so, they missed the point."

"Perhaps fortunately," Arisaydia murmured, turning his head toward the sound of her voice, the mask visible, apparently, to his memory. "But I was young and angry."

Penric accepted the object, turning it to check the side he cared about. It was made to cover the upper half of the face, and its dimensions closely matched the ravages of the scalding. No problem to pad it with ointment-saturated gauze, changeable according to each day's needs. And, while feigning to Arisaydia that it would hide his disfigurement from unsympathetic eyes, it would also keep the man from discovering prematurely what Penric had been doing to him, before the work was done.

What will we do in the after? Nikys had asked. Pen still had no answer, but the problem would soon be upon them all, and it wasn't going to be the one she was imagining.

Penric turned the mask over. The front side was black leather, cut and stitched in elegant lines, decorated with striking sprays of black feathers a little ragged and brittle from age and a sojourn in some chest. "And what did you go as?" he asked Nikys. "A swan?" White to her brother's dramatic black?

She laughed. "Not I! Even back then I had more sense. I went as an owl. A much rounder bird." She waved a hand down her body, which was indeed more owl- than swan-shaped. Pen thought she looked wonderfully soft, but he didn't suppose he dared say so.

"Wisdom bird," said Arisaydia. The ghost of a smile twitched his lips. "I remember that. Did I tease you?"

"Of course."

"Foolish raven."

Curious, Pen held up the mask before Arisaydia's face. And blinked.

"My word," said Des. Pen quickly closed his mouth before she could add more, and more embarrassing, commentary.

With the eye-diverting damage obscured, the man sprang into focus as not exactly handsome, but arrestingly powerful. Pen had met men and women like that, from time to time; it was nothing a sculptor could ever capture, not residing in the line or the form, but when one saw them, souls ablaze, one could not look away. The raven mask emphasized the effect, unfairly.

No, keep looking! Des demanded. *For all the stares you've been sneaking at his sister's ample backside, you can give us this. He's not going to object.*

They'd had this argument in bathhouses where, in general, Pen went because he wanted a bath. Seven-twelfths of Desdemona found the places fascinating for more prurient reasons, although not including, curiously, the imprint of the courtesan Mira, who knew more about what might be done in bathhouses—besides bathing—than Penric had ever imagined, and shared it whether

Pen wanted to know or not. Mira was professionally unimpressed with prurience. Some of the rest of the sorority were inclined to goggle—Pen swore Ruchia was the worst—which, since they seized Pen's eyes to do so, had a few times early on got him either punched or propositioned by his fellow bathers. Once, both.

You'd be propositioned anyway, Des objected. *That part is not our fault.*

Firmly, Penric set the mask aside. "That will work," he assured Nikys, keeping his eyes lifted. "Thank you." He was rewarded with another faint smile, like glancing moonlight.

A little later, when Nikys had gone off to see to preparations for the next meal, and Pen was working on modifying the mask, he judged Arisaydia sufficiently disarmed by their excursions into his family history to try more troubling questions. He definitely had to ask them before the return of Arisaydia's vision upended any belief that his secrets no longer mattered. *And you accuse me of being ruthless*, Des sniffed. Arisaydia had been apprised of the little fiction about his anonymous military benefactors, whose names Pen had steadfastly refused to divulge because they didn't exist, and he didn't dare make any up. But this had lent Pen a useful air of rectitude. Pen decided to deploy them again.

"Your secret friends who hired me were very upset with the rumors about your arrest," he started. "Outraged by some, worried, I think, by others. Did all this come out of nowhere, from your point of view?" Surely the general had been taken by surprise or he else could have fled, or flung up some other evasion or resistance.

"Not...nowhere," said Arisaydia slowly. He held out a hand palm-up, as if measuring some unseen threat. "Accusation and counter-accusation, rumor and slander, are staples of the Thasalon court, as men wrestle for advantage and access to the emperor's favor. I thought I was well out of it, and just as glad to be so, up here in Patos."

"Do you know who your enemies are?"

Arisaydia's laugh held little humor. "I could reel off a list. Although in this case, my friends were likely the greater danger."

"I...don't understand?" Pen scarcely needed to fake a confused naiveté.

"The Western Army was not well treated by Thasalon in our last campaign. Supplies and reinforcements were almost impossible to extract, pay was in arrears... In an offensive campaign, an army can pay itself out of the spoils of the enemy country. But we were defending, on our own ground. Pillage was discouraged and, when it occurred, complained of to the government. And punished, which set up its own tensions. In some encounters we were scarcely better organized than the barbarians we fought, and we were well-chewed by them. Our victory was more desperate than triumphal.

"The army always complains they are insufficiently rewarded for the burdens they undertake. It was more true than usual this time around, and the muttering in the tents and barracks fed on itself and turned ugly. There are invariably military men who believe if only they could replace whatever emperor is on the throne with one of their own, their injustices would be remedied."

"That seems to have been tried, judging by the histories I've read." And Pen had read rather more of them than he was going to let on, not that one could trust their writers. "Successfully, sometimes."

Arisaydia grimaced. "Ten years ago, even five years ago, I would have believed that myth wholeheartedly, that we needed only the right man to quell all wrongs. But, as you say, it's been tried, and nothing seems to change in the end. I had to see a lot more of the court to learn what we are up against, and it isn't just the corruption of courtiers, for all that we're well-supplied with that, too. Taxation is a mess, for one thing. The sporadic plagues have chewed holes in the fabric of the realm. At some golden periods the shortfall was made up for by conquest, I suppose, but it seems every generation we lose more territory than we gain. Reform is resisted by everyone who has an interest in it not taking place at *their* expense. Including the army, I'm sorry to say. To set one man, no matter how heroic or well-intentioned, up against the whole vast weight of that...and then to excoriate him for his inevitable failure..." He shook his head. "I would say *five gods spare me*, but there was a cadre of my officers who thought otherwise. And started to go beyond muttering. Evidently, half a year and Patos were not distance enough to save me from their admiration. And the reaction it engendered."

Arisaydia, Pen noticed, was naming no names, and likely not for the same reasons Pen hadn't. In his present state it seemed less calculation than habit, and a curious habit it was for a man to have developed.

"Did you not write to the duke of Adria asking for, um, greater distance? That was one of the rumors." Penric had held the letter in his hand in the duke's cabinet and read it. The chancellery of Adria was expert in forgeries, both detecting and creating them, but it had been in a scribe's handwriting, with only Arisaydia's signature appended. The duke had been frank with Pen about the dubious possibilities, which was why he'd been supposed to sound out the general most discreetly at first. And, should it not prove Arisaydia's idea, implant it anyway.

"Adria! Certainly not. Why would I treat with Adria? Their sea merchants are little better than pirates, sometimes. Rats with boats, nibbling at our coasts." Arisaydia's mouth set. He couldn't glower yet, but his eyelids tensed, and then his lips parted in pain. "Agh." He sighed and huddled down in his sheets, obviously tiring.

Well, that wasn't encouraging for Pen's secondary plan. He had begun to wonder, if he could restore Arisaydia's sight, if he might persuade him to flee east after all. Not that letting the duke aim Arisaydia at Carpagamo, a country that had never done harm to Pen, seemed a very holy mission, but politics were generally unholy, and that had never kept the Temple from dabbling in them. But he could not have stayed in Martensbridge and kept his sanity, and the archdivine of Adria had promised him a place that did not include duties to the Mother's Order.

Yet here I am, practicing medicine again all unwilled. Is the Bastard laughing?

This left the question of who in Cedonia had forged the initial letter, as the duke was fully convinced it had originated here. Clear entrapment, it seemed. Vicious both in its intent and its results. Velka might have brought it; he'd certainly escorted the very real reply back into the right wrong Cedonian hands, which had to have been outstretched waiting for it.

Penric was really starting to want some time alone in a quiet room with Velka. He was theologically forbidden to kill with his magic, but there were other possibilities. So very, very many. And oh gods he surely now understood why physician-sorcerers were the most tightly controlled of all the discreet cadre of Temple mages.

Desdemona couldn't lick her lips, but she could lick his. It brought him out of his furious fugue with a start. Her little frisson of anticipatory excitement faded, and she sighed.

Don't tempt me, and he had no idea which of them said it.

VIII

AS SHE AND the physician walked Adelis around the garden between them, just two days after he'd first been persuaded up, Nikys was pleased to see how much steadier he was on his feet. It was plain that the overwhelming pain of his scalding, so precisely and cruelly placed, that had driven him close to madness was vastly reduced. He was healing with amazing speed.

She did not know what mysterious Wealdean techniques the half-foreign physician was bringing to his task, but her respect for his skills had risen and risen. Even as he went on being rather odd. He talked to himself, for one thing, when he didn't think he was overheard, in what she guessed was his father's tongue, or sometimes in snatches of what she recognized as Darthacan. And then argued back. He always smiled at her, yet his bright eyes were restless and strained, as if masking a brain busy elsewhere.

As they turned and paced along the wall, Adelis unwound his arm from Master Penric's, but not from hers; his hand drifted up to touch his cheek just below the black mask. The sly design made him look strong, and dangerous, and not at all invalidish. It made him look quite like himself, in fact, at least when in one of his more sardonic moods. But his voice was uncharacteristically tentative as he asked, "Does my face look like a goat's bottom?"

Her heart clenched, but she returned lightly, "I always thought your face looked like a goat's bottom, dear brother. It appears no different to *me*."

Penric's brows lifted in concern as he turned to her across Adelis. But Adelis just smirked, looking mordant below the mask, and gave her arm a squeeze, returning in a matching tone, "Dear sister. Always my compass." His voice fell to quiet seriousness. "In the darkest places. It seems."

She swallowed and squeezed back.

Penric offered, "Your blisters looked much better this morning. Almost gone."

"Are you a connoisseur of blisters, Master Penric?" asked Adelis.

"It goes with my trade, I suppose. Yours were superb."

"That's Adelis for you," said Nikys. "Always has to have the best."

A huff of laugh. "Your latest ointment has tamed the itching, thankfully."

"Good. I don't want you scratching."

They turned once more and negotiated the steps up to the pergola, and Nikys said, "Go around again? Or rest?"

"Go around again," said Adelis, definitely. Nikys smiled.

But before they could continue, a brisk knocking at the front door echoed through the atriums, and they all paused, listening intently. The gardener-porter answered and admitted the supplicant. Supplicants; two voices quizzed him. If it was a friendly visit, it was the first since they'd been plunged into this political quarantine. If it was not...

A sharp, indrawn breath from Master Penric drew her attention. "I know that voice. One of them. I need—he mustn't see me!" The voices approached, the aged gardener shuffling slowly in escort, the others stepping impatiently short to match. Penric looked around frantically; he was quite cut off from the house by the visitors' entry route. "No time."

To Nikys's astonishment, he scrambled up the corner post of the pergola like a cat climbing a tree to escape a dog. He swung back down to add, "He's no friend to you. Be careful." And then ran lightly along the top, making the grape leaves bounce and quiver. Adelis, lips parted in unvoiced question, turned his head to track the thumps and rustles. Reaching the second-floor balcony overlooking the back garden, Penric vaulted over the railing and melted to the floor. Nikys could spot one blue eye peeking back through the uprights.

Uncertain, Nikys guided Adelis to the outdoor table. He seated himself stiffly. The porter and his charges arrived, a pair of men in civil dress followed by a sharply turned-out provincial guard. If Penric had recognized one voice, Nikys recognized one man: the provincial governor's senior secretary, Master Prygos. Neither friend nor enemy, she would have thought, just a punctilious functionary, his ambitions restricted to his own domain. The gray-haired, dyspeptic bureaucrat half-bowed to each of them, more habitually polite than truly respectful, as Adelis could not see it. Prygos cursorily introduced his trailing clerk as Tepelen. This was a younger man, shrewd-faced, evidently not in his trade long enough for his body to soften and grow pale like his superior's.

"I am charged today to deliver your copy of your bill of attainder," he told Adelis, formally. He nodded to Tepelen, who rummaged in his documents case and withdrew a thick sheaf, evidently a list of all the property Adelis no longer owned. Tepelen handed it to Prygos, who turned to hand it to Adelis, then paused and said, "Er."

Penric, by whatever impulse, had lined the eyeholes of the mask with a double layer of black silk, giving it an unsettling effect of gleaming bird eyes. The light played over the silk as Adelis nodded toward her. "Pray give it to Madame Khatai," he murmured. "She is my scribe these days."

"Ah. Yes."

Nikys took it, glanced through the cramped governmental calligraphy and legal cant, and set it down under her elbows.

Adelis inquired shortly of Prygos, "Do I have anything left to live on, or should I find a begging bowl for the marketplace?"

Prygos cleared his throat. "Madame Khatai's pension was left alone, as was the property of her mother that your mother left to her. Your dependents will not be houseless."

"Small mercies," said Adelis.

"They suffice," murmured Nikys. It would be a constrained little life, the pair of them crammed back into her aging mother's house in its small inland town. Betrayed. Defeated. *But not dead. Therefore, not hopeless.* Call it, in Adelis's lexicon, a retreat to regroup.

Prygos's hand rose, then fell; he looked to his clerk, who cast him a steely frown. He cleared his throat again, and said, "My apologies, but I am also charged to inspect and report on General Arisaydia's injuries and recovery." Adelis's military title was a slip, Nikys thought, unusual for so precise a man. "Uh, Madame Khatai, might I trouble you to help remove his mask?"

Adelis's jaw set; his hands clenched on the table-top. She let her own hand reach out to cover his fist in silent inquiry. Barely perceptibly, he shook his head. "If humiliation is to be my bread," he murmured to her, "best I grow accustomed to the taste."

She sighed, sickened, and rose to step behind him and unlace the strings holding his mask and dressings in place. She reached around him to lift it as gently as she had seen Master Penric do; she felt a slight tug as the ointment released, but his skin seemed much less fragile today. He didn't even flinch, reverting to that stubborn I-am-a-boulder stolidity.

Then he gasped.

She flitted instantly around to his side. "Oh, gods, did I hurt you?"

A flash of startled red gleamed between his shrunken lids as he turned his head toward her, then his eyes squeezed closed again. His hands tightened on the table's edge, knuckles paling. His teeth set and his body trembled. "Maybe a little," he managed.

She sank back down in her seat, setting the mask on the table. Prygos gulped and looked away. Tepelen, by contrast, sat up with a muffled oath. He leaned forward, eyes narrowing as he stared into the half-wreck of Adelis's face.

"Pray excuse us for just a moment." He rose, and his hand fell to Prygos's shoulder, gripping it, pressing him to rise and follow. Prygos looked up, surprised, but obeyed, and wasn't that odd? Tepelen motioned at the impassive guard, who had propped himself against the pergola post. "Stay. Keep them here." The two men trailed away through the house and out the front. Nikys pricked her ears, but neither spoke till the door closed between, cutting off sound.

"Nikys," said Adelis, his voice taut, "I'm getting a little tired. Perhaps you could escort me back up to my bedchamber."

"Of course."

She started to rise again, but the guard put in sternly, "Please stay seated, General."

Adelis's hands wavered out, found her, patted their way up to her head. He turned her face close to his. His eyes slitted open again. The whites were bloodshot nearly solid red, his irises were a strange garnet color, but the tight black circles of his pupils *looked back at her.* "Dear Nikys," he said. "In that case, perhaps you could fetch refreshments for our guests, and for me. Get my attendant to help you." The lids pinched closed once more, concealing...a terrible wonder. And an exactly equal terrible danger.

Her head felt so bloodless with shock that she feared she might pass out, but she said, "Certainly," and scrambled to her feet. The guard frowned, but evidently decided that her mouse-self, mere nurse-maid to the important man, was too frail a threat to concern him.

She walked firmly into the house, not looking back. She did not turn aside toward the kitchen, though she mentally reviewed the residue of wine in the pantry, fit only for servants and therefore too good for these visitors, and her stock of ready poisons, sadly lacking. She walked, did not run, *don't run*, up the stairs to the gallery. Master Penric was no longer lying prone on the back balcony, but she heard faint noises coming from Adelis's chamber.

She entered and closed the door behind her to find him swiftly packing the last of his medical kit. He'd pulled on trousers under his tunic. He looked up and cast her the most contrived smile yet.

Of the dozen alarms jostling her mouth, one escaped first: "He can see!"

"Yes."

"How long?"

"Since yesterday. Or if you mean when did I know I could recover his eyesight, since nearly the beginning, or I'd have been gone long ago."

She gaped at him. "Are you leaving now?"

"No...I don't know. I'm not *finished*." He grimaced and snapped his case closed. "More to the point, Velka saw. Worst possible time for the man to show up, I swear."

"Who?"

"Tepelen. The clerk who isn't. I don't know which is his real name. Maybe neither. He's a high-level agent from the cabal in the capital who entrapped your brother. I don't know how high, but he isn't stupid, and he doesn't waste time." He looked around. "And neither should we. Is there any money in this room? Anything Adelis or you would want to aid your flight from the city?"

She would cry *What flight?* but his intent, and their need, were too plain to argue. "We haven't enough coin left to pay the *laundress* tomorrow. I was hoping she would take something in trade."

"Can you ride?"

"Yes. But I haven't a horse."

"Hnh." He stood up and tapped his lips with his thumb. "I would so prefer to be discreet about this. May not be possible." They both froze as the sound of the front door slamming, and the tread of too many heavy feet, penetrated faintly from the atrium.

"Bastard's hell, no good. Go back and stay by your brother. I won't be far away. Don't panic."

If her glare could have blasted him where he stood, he would be floating ash. She whirled and ran for the stairs.

She made it back to the table barely before the new invasion. Prygos and his not-clerk were followed by four guardsmen, the two who'd been posted at her doors and two more. The one who'd been left on watch pushed off from his pergola support and looked his inquiry not at the senior secretary, but at Tepelen. Or Velka. Or whoever the cursed man was.

Tepelen gestured at Adelis. "Seize and bind him."

Adelis's chair banged over backward as he surged up out of it. No question of tame surrender this time. Nikys realized too late that she should have detoured by the kitchen to grab a carving knife, or two, but she snatched up her own chair and used it to charge at least one of the men. She caught him so by surprise she actually managed to knock him backwards, but he grabbed the legs and yanked and nearly took her down with him. When she tried to stomp him with her feet, he clutched her ankle and toppled her. She landed painfully, the world spinning, and then he seized her hair.

Adelis was more adept, and more professionally vicious, but the four other guardsmen and Tepelen combined against him. And while it was plain he could see *something* now, it was equally plain his sight must still be blurred and indistinct, and when one of the men managed a hard blow against his tender upper face, he gasped and staggered, and then they were all upon him.

She and Adelis both struggled and fought to the last, but the last came swiftly when swords were drawn. They were roped tightly to two opposite pergola posts, panting and bruised, staring at each other in dismay. And where was Master Penric and his promises in all this? Not that the skinny physician could have been much more help in a fight than she had been, but he might have dropped the odds against Adelis from five down to four.

Tepelen, out of breath, huffed upright and straightened his clothes. Prygos, who had stood back from the brawl in understandable terror, came up to his side, and both approached the bound Adelis. Adelis's head jerked back as Prygos lifted his hand to touch his burns.

"As you said," Prygos remarked, apparently to Tepelen. "The man who administered the vinegar must not have had his heart in the task. Someone is going to have to question him, later."

"He seemed diligent to me," Adelis gritted between his teeth. His mouth was bleeding, but then, so was Nikys's. She licked the metallic tang from her swelling lips. "But by all means, feel free to question him. To the last extremity."

"Enough of this," said Tepelen. "Let us amend the lapse and go. No merit in dragging it out. The fine judicial show was all over a week ago." He gestured to a guard. "You—no, you two—hold his head still." Two guardsmen came up to either side of Adelis and grasped his head. The tendons stood out on Adelis's neck as he strained against their hands, and his breath whistled through his teeth. Prygos stepped well back, gesturing assent though looking rather ill. Tepelen grimaced in distaste, drew his belt knife, and raised it toward Adelis's eyes.

Nikys screamed.

"Oh, now," came a soft voice from above. "I really can't allow that."

For no reason that Nikys could see, Tepelen hissed and dropped the knife as though it seared him. Clutching his hand, he whirled and stepped back to look up.

Master Penric stood atop the end of the pergola above Adelis's head, one hand cocked on his hip, looking peeved.

Tepelen's jaw dropped in disbelief. "You! You're supposed to be drowned!"

"Really?" Penric's head tilted as he contemplated this. "Perhaps I was."

Horror flashed in the man's face, to be replaced swiftly with dawning anger. His mouth clopped closed, opening again to shout to the bewildered guardsmen, "Seize him!"

That sounding a more reasonable order, they all started forward. Penric's features set in a look of inward concentration, and one pale hand waved, fingers tapping like a man directing a group of musicians. One after another, the five guardsmen dropped to the floor with cries of pain, their legs sprawling out every which way, helpless to stand as a new foal. Tepelen lurched and followed them down.

Prygos, his eyes bulging, yelped and turned to run.

Penric bent to gaze after him. "Oh. Forgot about you." He waved his hand again, and the secretary tripped and fell, seeming unable to get up again, although he attempted to row himself along the floor with his arms, casting terrified looks over his shoulder.

Penric heaved a sigh and climbed down from the pergola. His face shifted and he vented a weird, silent laugh. "So much for discreet, Penric." He strode among the guardsmen, now flopping feebly like dying fish, and kicked swords away. As he bent to touch each man's throat, their cries squeezed to squeaks, although his hand drew back from Tepelen's, who was the only man not screaming. "Not you, yet."

All the clamor died away. Nikys's ears rang with the silence. Penric stood up straight. He grimaced and gestured again, and the ropes binding Nikys and Adelis to their respective posts loosened and dropped around their feet.

Nikys thudded to her knees. Adelis staggered forward, grasped Penric by the shirt, and slammed him up against another post. His face was wild, and not just from his squinting, bright red eyes, as he shoved into Penric and cried—wailed, almost—"*What are you?*"

"Now, now." Penric favored him with his sunniest grin. "Mustn't look a gift horse in the mouth."

"That's not an answer!" He shook the physician, who allowed himself to flop bonelessly, unresisting.

Nikys suspected him capable of resisting very effectively indeed, if he chose.

Shaking, she used her post to haul herself to her feet, and rubbed at her bleeding mouth, her numb jaw. "Why didn't you let us loose sooner?" *Or do* anything *sooner?*

"I thought about it, but it would have put one random element too many in an already complicated situation. Our attention does have limits. Actually safer to leave you where you were, temporarily." As Adelis released him with a curse, he brushed down his scarcely rumpled green jacket, and stretched like a cat. His mouth didn't stop smiling, but the smile didn't reach his eyes, which flickered constantly over the scene of not-exactly-slaughter.

Adelis seemed intent on correcting that, as he bent and snatched up a sword.

Penric's hand fell atop his. "No, you can't kill them. They're helpless, you know."

"*So was I.*"

Penric gave him a conceding nod, but said, "You have a more urgent task right now. You have to get your sister to safety."

Nikys, who'd been frantically wondering how she was to get *Adelis* to safely, was offended by this blatant tactic, but it worked; her brother's head cranked around to find her. *Reminded of my existence, are you?* Granted, Penric was a very distracting man. Adelis, still gripping the sword, hurried over to hug her to him.

"Are you all right, Nikys?"

"Just knocked around."

He glared thinly down at the guardsmen, as if reconsidering his prey. But, stepping over the bodies—Adelis kicked a few in passing—Penric hurried them both into the atrium, lowering his voice.

"There are two horses tethered outside. Madame Khatai, if you have riding trousers, go put them on. Grab whatever moneys you have, no more clothes or treasures than will fit in a sack, and be back down here as fast as if the house was burning."

"The house isn't burning." Though it felt as if her life were on fire.

"Yet."

Compelled by his infectious insanity, she ran. A stack of cloth and his medical case were already sitting at the bottom of the stairs, she noticed as she galloped up them.

She returned to find Penric belting one of her longer gowns around a hotly protesting Adelis.

He then pulled her widow's green cloak off its peg and settled it around her brother's shoulders, and yanked the hood up over his head. "There. Your magical cape of invisibility. Keep your face down."

Penric peered out the front door, then bundled them into the quiet street, dozing in the bright afternoon. He gave her a leg up onto the larger of the two horses, both marked with provincial government brands and bearing military saddles. A short delay followed while he argued in sharp whispers with Adelis about the widow's clutch on the sword, settled by sliding it semi-discreetly back into its saddle scabbard, but inciting another dispute about getting him up behind her.

"There are two horses," said Adelis. "One for each of us."

"You are not as fit to ride as you think you are, which you are going to find out shortly when the excitement wears off, and there are three of us. I need the other to follow on."

"You're coming with us?" asked Nikys. She could scarcely describe her own reaction. Though not *sorry*, no.

The blond man nodded. "I wasn't done yet, you see. Leave town at a sedate walk, nothing to draw attention to yourselves—not to mention easier on this poor horse—and take the south road. I have a few things to deal with here, and then I'll catch up to you."

"How will you find us?"

"I can find you."

"You and who else?" began Adelis in exasperation.

Further protest was cut short when Penric stepped back and slapped the horse on its haunches, Nikys found her reins, and they...fled at an amble.

They were both quiet for a little, as the reverberations of terror running through Nikys's heart slowly died away. She could barely imagine how Adelis felt about it all, twice-betrayed as he was. She could sense it, though, as the fight began to leak out of him and he leaned more heavily against her.

They'd threaded through three streets and found the main road before Nikys said, "I wonder if he really means to burn down the villa?"

After a brief consideration, Adelis offered, "It's rented."

"I should be sorry anyway." And then, "What in the gods' eyes did we see him *do*, back there?"

Adelis's voice went grim. "Something uncanny."

"Hedge sorcerer? Do you think? You saw him more nearly than I."

"It would explain a great deal. In retrospect."

But why had such a man come to them? She considered Penric's airy tale of their military benefactors with a new dubiousness, but she had no better one to put in its place. His brief, bizarre first exchange with Tepelen also hung without explanation. "Do you think he'll really catch up to us?"

"No. He'd be a fool to. Far smarter to take this chance of escape to safety."

She considered what *safety* might mean to a man who could do the things they'd just witnessed, and wondered.

Also, *fool*.

IX

$\mathcal{P}$ENRIC DASHED BACK through the house, trying to track all he must control. *Too much.* In addition to the assailants laid out under the pergola, and the whining senior secretary, the maid and the porter were presently cowering in an upstairs room, and the scullion had vanished. Well, first things first, then whatever else he could do, and then fly.

He passed through and collected all the weapons, not forgetting the secretary's belt knife and also taking a moment to harvest his purse. Then he renewed the pressure on his prisoners' selected nerves to keep them down and quiet. He didn't suppose anyone else would appreciate how *delicate* and *clever* all this was, least of all his victims, but he was rather proud of it himself. *Good work.*

I could have ripped all those nerves apart much *more easily*, grumped Des, *and we'd never have to worry about them getting up to come after us again.*

Which was true, but theologically fraught. Penric dumped his heavy armload of edged steel down the privy at the end of the garden and trotted back to the pergola. The soldiers lay in whimpering heaps. One brave man made a feeble snatch for his ankle as Pen skipped around them, but missed. Pen grasped the panting Velka-Tepelen-Whoever—he decided he'd stick with Velka—by the tunic and began dragging him into the house. There were already too many witnesses to his antics. This conversation needed to be private.

A sort of lumber room off the front atrium seemed remote enough to be out of earshot. Penric laid Velka out supine on the floor and perched on his abdomen, knees up, and touched his thumb to his lips in his habitual prayer for luck. His god, he was reminded, was the master of both sorts. He leaned forward between his up-folded legs and smiled.

"Drowned, you say," he began. Des growled aloud in memory.

"The guards reported you drowned in your cell and your body disposed of in the sea," said Velka through his teeth. "Your skull was broken. You *should* be dead. Twice over!"

"And Arisaydia should be blind, aye. So many mysteries."

"No mystery to it. You escaped, and they reported the other to hide their failure and avoid punishment."

"Well, that's one explanation. But wouldn't it be more interesting if they were speaking the truth?"

Velka glared. This was not a man inclined to babble in fear, alas. Or talk much at all.

"There is so much I could do to you," mused Pen. "Take your hearing, as you plunged me into silence in that cell…" He leaned forward and cupped both hands over Velka's ears, then moved them to cover his eyes. "Or your vision, as you plunged me into darkness." He sat up again, palms on his knees. "Who is your master?"

"Who is yours?" Velka shot back. "The duke of Adria?"

"Ultimately, no," said Pen judiciously. "He just borrowed me. And when you borrow a valuable tome from a friend, it doesn't do to carelessly drop it in the privy. But enough of that." It occurred to him that anyone following up from Adria on Pen's disappearance would be most likely to encounter the official tale, at least until he could make his way back to gainsay it, and believe him dead. *Bastard's tears, what will happen to my books?*

Pen, he's getting more out of this than you are, complained Des. *Attend!*

"So which shall it be? Ears?" Pen clapped them, but did nothing destructive. He tried to replicate Velka's own look of bored distaste when he'd lifted his knife to Arisaydia's face, while simultaneously mustering the intense concentration needed to compress one of the body's most elegant nerves without permanently damaging it. He suspected he just came out looking constipated. "Or"—he moved one hand over Velka's left eye, made carefully sure of his invisible target, *pinched*—"your remaining eye?"

Velka's scream of anguish was entirely sincere, Pen thought. Despite the pain already placed in his body blocking his range of movement, he tried to thrash under Pen, his head whipping back and forth, and Pen was thrust in his imagination back to the scene of Arisaydia and the boiling vinegar. He hoped Velka was, too.

Pen leaned forward again, and hissed, "*Who is your master?*"

"Minister Methani," gasped Velka.

Methani was prominent in the first circle of men around the emperor, and from a high and wealthy family, Pen recalled from his readings and conversations back in Adria; he didn't know offhand if the man was one of those who had volunteered, or been volunteered, for emasculation so as to rise in imperial trust, or not. Pen's lips pursed in bafflement. "Why would he want to destroy his emperor's most effective general? Seems treasonous in itself to me. Not to mention grossly wasteful."

Velka wheezed, "Arisaydia was a danger to us all. Too independent. Too attractive. Already military conspiracies were starting to swirl about him. We couldn't penetrate the intrigues that had to be reaching him, so we made one to serve in their place."

Which was...pretty much what Arisaydia had said. For all his theatrics, Pen didn't feel he was moving forward, here. Though he wondered if that *too independent* translated to *wouldn't lie down under the thumbs of the right men.*

"Didn't it occur to any of you people that the reason you couldn't find a line was that there wasn't one? That you weren't destroying a disloyal man, but creating one?"

"If he wasn't disloyal yet, he was ripe to fall," Velka snarled back. "And then the cost of stopping him would be much higher."

Well, one couldn't say Velka didn't believe in his mission. Not the wholly cynical tool of some wholly cynical master, quite.

Cynical enough, said Des. *Spies have to be.*

I suppose you would know. Ruchia.

A touch. Des aimed a grimace at him, and subsided.

"Also," Pen added a bit more tartly, "if you didn't treat your armies so badly in the first place, they wouldn't go out looking for some poor sod to stick up on a standard in front of them and fight you for their favor. It doesn't seem to me the root of this is *Arisaydia's* fault. It's, it's, it's…just your own masters' *bad management.* Circling back to bite them. If you'd spend half this effort fixing the real problems, you could stop all the disaffected generals before they started, instead of, of blinding them piecemeal one by one. You're worse than evil. You're *inefficient.*"

Velka stared at him through his one good eye, so taken aback he stopped whimpering. "What are you really sent to Cedonia for?"

"I'm beginning to wonder," Penric admitted ruefully. If he was sent to be *Velka's* spiritual advisor, it seemed a supremely unfunny joke on Someone's part. Which didn't make it unlikely.

He also thought of the unexpected treasury found in the Father of Winter's offering box in the temple. *Maybe the duke of Adria wasn't the only one who has borrowed me?* The suspicion was simultaneously heartening and horrifying.

The Father wasn't Penric's god, but He might be Velka's. "Do you have children?" he asked, then, at Velka's flinch, added hastily, "No, don't tell me. I don't want to know."

Revenge was tempting, but not his mandate.

I don't know why not, said Des. *Arisaydia was ready to slay them all, and leave no witnesses.* A sense of reluctant admiration. No…not reluctant.

You know we can't do that.

I *can't, with our sorcery.* You *could, with your right arm, if you hadn't thrown all the blades down the jakes.*

Penric decided to ignore this. He sat up, considering his congregation of one.

"My time is short," he said at last, "so my sermon will be, too. When a man witnesses a miracle of the gods, the prudent first response should not be to try to *undo* it." A long finger reached out to tap Velka between the eyes; he jerked back. It had actually been a lot of meticulous, tricky, uncomfortable chaos-sluffing uphill sorcery, but Velka didn't need to know that. Though given Desdemona's ultimate source, perhaps it was true after a fashion. "So consider me a messenger from a higher power than a duke, and let me help you to remember this. To use the machineries of justice to commit injustice is the deepest offense to the Father of Winter."

He pressed his thumb to the middle of Velka's forehead. As he knew so well from his mountain childhood, cold could burn as brutally as fire. The work was vastly finer than his ice floe, not nearly as subtle as the labor he'd been doing all week. He lifted his thumb to reveal thin, frozen white lines in the shape of a stylized snowflake, surrounded by a red bloom of hurt. It would heal, ultimately, to a red then a white brand on Velka's skin.

It didn't come close to the amount of scarring Arisaydia would bear. But as a pointed memento, Pen fancied this wintery mark might serve.

He dismounted from Velka, collected the man's purse to keep company with that from the provincial secretary, and pressed himself to his feet, suddenly very tired. Time to go.

Past time, Des agreed.

As he made for the door, Velka wrenched himself around on the floor and cried, "Hedge sorcerer! You're *insane!*"

Your fine sermon doesn't seem to have taken, Learned Penric, said Des. She was much too amused.

Pen took two steps out, aiming to collect his medical case and his soon-to-be-stolen horse, then whipped around. He stuck his head through the lumber room door and yelled back, "I'm not a *hedge* sorcerer. And your government policies are *stupid!*"

He was still fuming when he rode to the end of the street. From the edge of his eye, he caught a glimpse of the scullion coming back, leading a pelting posse of guardsmen. Which answered the question of who had been the spy among Madame Khatai's servants, he supposed, rather too late to do any practical good. He pressed his horse into a quick trot, rounding the corner safe from their view.

X

———————————

"WE NEED TO be moving faster," said Adelis. Although the way his chin had sunk to Nikys's shoulder suggested he was growing as fatigued as their doubly burdened horse. They'd come about twelve miles out of Patos, she guessed.

The traffic had thinned from the bustle around the city, where they'd threaded their way past builders' ox-carts, donkeys laden with vegetables for the markets, animals being driven to the butchers, sedan chairs and open chariots, and private coaches whose drivers had shouted them out of the path. They'd passed a road-repair crew whose lewd catcalls at the two unescorted women had made Adelis growl, his hand twitching for his sword, and, once, a troop of soldiers marching the other way, which had made him hunch and lower his face, squinting sidewise from the shadow of the hood trying to make out markers of regiment and rank.

Out here, fellow travelers had dwindled to the occasional farm wain or herdsman with pigs. The sun was slanting across the countryside, spreading buttery light over the small farms and larger villas tracking the watercourses, the grapevines and flickering gray-green olive groves on the slopes, the rocky heights given over to scrub and goats and sheep.

"We're moving faster than your army."

"*Anything* would move faster than an army," he returned. The spurt of remembered aggravation gave him the energy to sit up, at least.

"How are you bearing up back there?" She hesitated. "How much can you see?"

"It's…blurry. I can see colors. It's too bright. Makes my eyes water. Your cloak is too hot."

"Yes, I know." She felt oddly glad to be out of it. She'd once imagined the widow's green would protect her from unwanted attention, but there'd proved to be a certain cadre of men who imagined it marked her as available to them, instead. She'd quickly learned not to be unduly gentle in repelling their advances, and had held her borders where she wanted them. Of course, she'd always been backed by the tacit garrison of Adelis's rank and reputation—that, too, now attainted. She added, "Faster to where?"

"I'm thinking about that."

She said tentatively, "I was wondering if we should try to make for my mother's." In which case, they needed to find a different road.

"Five gods, no."

She glanced over her shoulder to catch his grimace.

"It's one of the first places they'll think to look, and harboring me would bring disaster down upon her." He paused. "You could probably take refuge there unmolested."

She answered this with the long, unfavorable silence it deserved. He evidently took her point, for his return grunt was muted.

He'd been alternating between keeping his face down and his eyes closed, trying to protect their inflamed sensitivity, and looking around, testing and retesting his returning sight as if fearful it would vanish away again. She interrupted this cycle to ask, "Did you realize Master Penric was uncanny? I mean, before that unholy show in the garden."

"I...as physicians went, he seemed more sensible than most. He had a trick of massaging my scalp that he said was for headache, and it certainly seemed to work. I don't know." He seemed to consider. "He could have been lying. About the healing, I mean. Perhaps I was not so badly injured as it felt like."

"No. I saw your face when he first lifted off the prison wrap. You were that badly injured." *And then some.*

He added somewhat inconsequently, "He didn't look like what I'd imagined. From his speech, I never guessed he'd be barely out of his youth." He peered around again, and stiffened.

"Pursuit?" asked Nikys. Could they get off the road and hide?

"In a manner of speaking."

She stood in her stirrups to look, but then eased back when she recognized the single horseman, puffs of pale dust kicking up in his wake on the dirt track that ran alongside the paved military road. In a few minutes, Master Penric trotted up beside them, both he and his horse sweating and winded. His face was flushed pink under a countryman's straw hat.

"Ah, good! I caught up with you."

"If it was that easy for you," said Adelis, "it will be that easy for them."

"Ah, probably not right away. They'll be quite a while sorting themselves out back there. And I had the advantage of knowing which road to try." He smiled cheerily, but it won him only dual glowers of suspicion. "But they know what they're dealing with in me now, which is, mm, unfortunate. Doubt they'll come so unprepared again."

"You didn't kill them while you could," said Adelis. It wasn't a question. "You left witnesses."

"Well, really, that would have been a problem. Would you have had me slay the maid and the porter, too? The scullion? The laundress? The butcher's lad? How about the apothecary...?"

Adelis scowled and looked away, discomfited.

"Take heart," Penric advised. "The next best thing to no witnesses is many, who will all contradict each other. Or else arrive at a consensus that has more to do with their needs than with what they've seen."

"Did you burn down the villa?" Nikys asked, thinking morbidly of her good floor loom, left behind along with so many of the tools of her life.

"What? Oh. No."

"So was his name Velka or Tepelen?"

"You know, I forgot to ask. He was the same man as—" Penric broke off, smiled, waved a hand as if to drive off a fly.

"Same man as who?" asked Adelis.

"Doesn't matter. He did say his master was a Minister Methani. Does that name mean something to you?"

Adelis shrugged. "Methani? Yes, that's very likely."

Penric looked disappointed at this tepid response. "Not a surprise, I take it."

"Not especially. We've been clashing at court for a couple of years, now."

"Had you ever done anything to anger him personally? Traduce his mother, steal his slippers, ravish his goat?"

Adelis cleared his throat. "I may have said a few intemperate things. From time to time."

Nikys snorted. She looked again sidelong at the strange blond man. "So you're really a sorcerer?"

Was he really a physician, for that matter? "Why did you follow after us?"

He lifted a hand from his reins and tilted it back and forth. "A number of reasons. Mostly because I hadn't finished treating your brother's eyes. It was upsetting to be so close to bringing off...what I mean to bring off, and be so rudely interrupted."

Adelis blew out a non-laugh, short and sardonic.

Penric turned in his saddle and added to him, "Also, I promised Des I would try to restore your eyebrows. She was rather set on it."

"Des?" said Adelis, beating Nikys to the question.

"Ah, ha, Desdemona, my demon. I suppose it's about time you were all introduced, given she's been living with you right along, within me, for the past week." He looked at them both, hopefully. "You do know that it's the acquisition, the possession, of a chaos demon that turns a person into a sorcerer, yes?"

Nikys didn't think she'd reacted visibly, but their horse yawed farther from Penric's.

Adelis said warily, "Is it...ascendant? That's a great danger for hedge sorcerers, I've heard."

"No, certainly not. I mean, yes, it's a significant hazard, but it's not the case here."

"How can you tell?" said Adelis. "That is…how can we tell?"

"A sorcerer or sorceress whose demon has become ascendant will exhibit far more chaotic—erratic—behavior."

A long silence. Twin, level stares.

Penric seemed stung. "No, really, not! Though Des does leak out from time to time. You've both heard her speak. With my voice, of course. It would be quite unkind to keep her wholly prisoned."

Adelis said slowly, "You…share your body…with this unnatural being?"

"Share and share alike, yes. It's an intimate relationship."

Adelis looked revolted; Penric was beginning to look offended by his reaction.

Nikys put in hastily, "It seems natural to me. Every mother does it, and every unborn child. Even Adelis and I once had to share another's body and blood."

"Unmanly, then," Adelis muttered.

Penric touched his thumb to his lips and gave a little bow in his saddle. "There are compensations. As you…can see." His thin smile put the point to the wordplay.

Nikys tried again to divert the tension: "Did Adelis's officers know you were a sorcerer when they hired you for him?"

"Ah, not exactly. By the way, do you know how far we are from the nearest largish town? Because we would be more remarked in a small village. And I'd prefer to find some inn that's quiet and clean to continue the eye treatments tonight."

"Doara is about eight miles off," said Nikys. "We should be there by sunset."

"Perfect. That will be a good time to get rid of these incriminating horses, too."

"You have a plan for that?" said Adelis, sounding distrustful.

"Oh, yes."

THEY WERE in sight of Doara, and dusk was closing in, when Master Penric pulled them off the road into the cover of some scrubby trees and had them dismount.

"I believe the best, and most confusing, thing will be to send these beasts back to their own stable. Better than just turning them loose to be found along our route."

As Adelis detached the saddle scabbard, Penric unbridled his mount, scratched its ears, and began rubbing its forehead, crooning under his breath in a strange tongue. Turning away to secure the bridle to the saddle, he remarked, "I once spent a year in Easthome, the capital of the Weald, studying their style of magic with the Royal Fellowship of Shamans. A geas of persuasion doesn't come at all naturally to a chaos demon, but we learned to simulate it. A real shaman can lay a geas lasting weeks or months. The best I can do is hours. Well, it's only a horse, and the compulsion lies in line with its own inclinations. I expect this will do."

He repeated the mystifying performance with the other animal, then turned them both loose with friendly slaps to their haunches. "Off you go, now." They snuffled and trotted away down the road together. "Ah." He bent over, looking distracted. A patter of wet red fell from his sunburned nose into the dry dirt.

"You're bleeding," said Nikys uneasily, wondering if she should fetch him a cloth out of her sack. She would have to sacrifice one of her few garments.

"Yes," he said, muffled. "Don't be alarmed. It will stop in a moment. A sorcerer pays for magic, uphill

magic, in some greater amount of disorder. A shaman pays in blood. The shedding of which, I argue,
is also a form of disorder. Shaman Inglis and I tried
to work out the implications of that..." He glanced
up to check their reactions. Nikys leaned forward,
a hand tentatively raised but with no idea what she
could do. Adelis had retreated a pace, the tree guard-
ing his back, fists clenched. "Ah, I might as well be
talking in Wealdean to you, I suppose. Never mind."

The gush tailing away, Penric rubbed his upper
lip with the back of his hand, straightened, and
smiled rather flatly. "Let's go find that inn. I'm
tired, aren't you?"

AT A lodging place on a side street in Doara, Master
Penric negotiated for two adjoining rooms, while
Adelis kept his head down in surly silence and
pretended to be a stout, standoffish widow. The awk-
wardness of concealing the sword under the cloak
lent him a convincing aged hunch. The moment their
chamber door shut behind them he shucked out of
the cloak and Nikys's dress, tossing them aside with
a muffled oath. Nikys rescued her abused clothing and nobly refrained from comment. Feigning

that his female employer's widowed mother was ill, Penric had arranged for their dinner to be brought up, which happened thankfully soon. It was eaten mostly in tense silence.

After the meal was cleared away from the small table, Penric, growing serious, laid out his medical kit and turned at last to Adelis. He first carefully cleaned away the day's grime from his patient's face, a sticky mess from the ointment, sweat, and road dust, and from around his eyes, but Nikys didn't think it was just from the firm touch that Adelis flinched away.

Penric evidently didn't think so either, for he said lightly, "Oh, come now. I've been helping you to your chamber pot for a week. If you trusted me in the darkness, you can trust me in the light."

Adelis grunted and, rigidly, endured the ministrations. After a while, he said, "You're a hedge sorcerer."

"Something like that."

"With a talent for healing."

Penric's voice went dryer. "Something like that."

"Not a physician at all."

"I said I'd taken no oath. It's…complicated. And not relevant here."

Nikys, seated closely and watching it all, said, "I would like to understand."

Penric hesitated, then shrugged. "Two of my demon's prior riders—possessors—were Temple-trained physicians. Their knowledge came to me as part of the same gift as their languages. Plus what I've added myself since acquiring Desdemona. Which she will carry on in turn someday to a new rider, after my death, which is a strange thought. Rather more useful than being a ghost, sundered souls not being good for much. They mostly won't even talk to you."

Nikys blinked at this last offhand observation; Adelis shifted his swollen red eyes.

"Have you tried to talk to ghosts?" she couldn't help asking.

"A few times. One feels they could answer so many questions, starting with *Who killed you?* but they almost never do." Standing behind the seated Adelis, Penric spread his fingers over his patient's scalp and paused in his chatting, though he sent her a faint smile evidently meant to be reassuring.

Nikys thought about all she'd seen. "Why do you call this...creature of chaos *her*?"

"Desdemona's prior ten human riders all chanced to be women. Plus the lioness and the mare, however you count them, but that goes back to her very beginnings. Right here in Cedonia, as it happens. This resulted over time—two hundred years of time—in a sort of composite personality that I named Desdemona, when she came down to me." His gaze grew pensive. "Your first gift to me, Penric. Though not your last."

Nikys, listening to the subtle shifts in his tone, was torn between fear and fascination. Had he always been doing this, disregarded? "Could—could I talk to her? Directly?"

Penric stared in surprise over Adelis's head. "I don't think anyone has ever asked us that before." His lips twitched. "Well, why not?"

Nikys swallowed, looked him in the eyes, and tried, "Hello…Desdemona."

Penric's smile transmuted to something more bemused. "Hello, Nikys."

"So…so you really live inside Master Penric? Like another person?"

"Or another dozen persons. It is our nature."

"How long, um, have you been…in there?" It felt absurdly like asking a new neighbor, *So, how long have you lived in Patos?*

"Since he was nineteen, and stopped to help my former mistress, Learned Ruchia, when she fell mortally ill upon a roadside in the cantons. Ruchia called him the Bastard's last blessing. We…thought we needed to learn what better to do about bad hearts."

"How long have you been together, then?" As if the neighbors were a married couple.

"Eleven, twelve years?" Master Penric—or was it the demon?—waved a dismissive hand.

To be certain the man wasn't just having an arcane jape at her expense, Nikys supposed she should think of some question to which the demon would know the answer and Penric would not, but none at once occurred to her. *Do you like being a demon? Is Penric a good master? What is it like to live for centuries?* Not to mention, *What was it like to be a woman, and then a man?* Did demons even think that way? She tried for something that seemed more answerable. "Why is Master Penric—Penric—not a proper physician?"

His expression seemed to conduct a brief war with itself, but he—or she?—replied, "A good question, child, but not mine to answer. Though if he ever does explain, you'll know he's come to trust you." His voice went sharper. "I think that's enough, Des."

Adelis, still sitting stiffly, rolled his eyes as best he could, as though he considered this offering dubious coin, and his sister a gull for accepting it. Nikys, watching those long fingers barely move through her brother's hair, wondered if she was witnessing some delicate sorcery being done right now. By Penric's abstraction, maybe so?

But Adelis, after a while, had a question of his own. "Can you kill with your demon magic?"

Penric grimaced—yes, this was Penric again now, and was this going to be like learning to tell two identical twins apart? "No."

"Fight?"

"Within limits. Did you think all those soldiers trying to arrest you earlier today tripped over their own boots?"

"What if your attackers were more than you could overcome?"

"Running away is always my first choice. After that, disable and run away. As you saw."

"What if you were truly cornered? A you-or-him contest?"

Penric's eyebrows pinched. "You've killed in warfare, presumably."

Adelis nodded shortly.

"Have you ever murdered? Slain one helpless before you?"

Adelis shrugged. "There were cleanups on the battlefield. More speeding a death already underway than a killing. Not a pretty business, nor heroic, but needful sometimes."

Penric, after a thoughtful moment, gave a conceding nod, and said, "I suppose. But every death, howsoever accomplished, opens a doorway to the gods. If I die, my soul goes to my god, if He'll have me. But should my demon murder, whether under my command or ascendant and rogue, she would be stripped from me through the victim's soul-door by her holy Master, her two hundred years of life and knowledge boiled back down to formless chaos in an instant. Worse than burning down a great library. So my mortal calculation is never just me or him. It's me or him or *her*. Do you see the conundrum?"

"...No."

"Imagine...I don't know, imagine Nikys was your demon. And, in slaying, would be not just slain but sundered. Could you see it then?"

Reluctantly, Adelis said, "Maybe. I see that you would lose your powers."

"And thus, I run away."

Adelis, his head drooping, vented a little unconceding huff, but did not pursue the matter further.

He did revive to protest when Penric made to place his mask—and when had he retrieved it?—relined with clean gauze and ointment, upon him for the night. "If you want to end up with working eyelids, you'll cooperate," said Penric sternly, and overbore him. Nikys didn't think he'd succeed in doing that for much longer.

When he'd finished cleaning up and restoring his supplies in their case, Penric told her, "I'm going out for a little."

"Why? You did that every night back at the villa, and I wondered."

"Ah." He paused at the door. "It's not a great mystery, if you recall what I told you of the price of uphill magic. Creating order, such as in healing, generates a greater burden of chaos, which I must promptly find a place to shed. The more efficiently I work out ways to do this, the more uphill magic I can safely accomplish."

"Wait. Does working this, these healings put you at some risk?"

"Not necessarily," he said cheerfully, and whisked out the door, shutting it firmly behind him.

"Not *necessarily*," she echoed aloud, hovering somewhere between baffled and peeved. "That's no answer!"

"If you haven't yet noticed that the man is as slippery as a fish," Adelis remarked dryly from his bed, "it's time you did. Also mad as a boot."

"Fish," Nikys returned with what dignity she could muster, "don't wear boots." It wasn't much of a rejoinder, nor much of a rebuttal, but it served to see her off to her own room.

XI

ARISAYDIA'S EYES LOOKED better the next morning, and saw better, too, Penric judged. Also more shrewdly, although that wasn't the eyes, exactly. For the first time, he refused even the reduced dose of the syrup of poppies, and insisted that his sister, not Penric, shave him. Which suggested he hadn't quite wrapped his military mind around how little a medically trained sorcerer needed a weapon, but it was perhaps not prudent to point this out.

Working the lather and razor carefully around the nearly healed burns, Nikys asked, "Will the brown come back?" Arisaydia's irises were still that peculiar deep garnet color, although the whites were clearing to merely a wine-sick sort of bloodshot.

"I'm not sure. I've never done a healing this delicate before." Pen didn't know if anyone had.

This triggered Arisaydia's demand for a mirror, which Nikys had to go fetch from the innkeeper's wife downstairs. It was good silvered glass, though, and its small circle reflected back a clear image of half of Arisaydia's face at a time. "Huh," he said, frowning and tilting it this way and that, but he seemed much less appalled than Penric had feared. Pen supposed the man had witnessed injuries more devastating than this in the course of his career. "I can work with this."

Without Pen's labors, the upper half of his face would have become a knotted mass of yellow, ropy scar tissue, but, of course, without Pen's labors Arisaydia would never have been troubled by the sight of it. These scars would eventually work out as flatter, paler, with redder skin between, in a sort of spray pattern not unlike an owl's feathers. Strange, but nothing to make children scream, and any woman who would recoil likely wasn't tough enough for Arisaydia anyway. Nikys managed to seem completely unruffled, a mirror Arisaydia had to find more reassuring than the glass one.

He emphatically refused to redon the blinding mask, so Penric made do with gauze wrappings above and below his eyes, which gleamed out like coals. By tomorrow, even those light dressings might be dispensed with. Pen's efforts last night had been intense, but the results were at last making themselves visible to less subtle senses than his own.

The other advantage to stopping at a larger town was that it could support a public livery, which Pen had located when he'd been out shedding chaos. Arisaydia made no objection to Pen's proposal to hire a private coach to carry them all farther south, which doubtless meant that he harbored his own ideas about their route in that direction that he wasn't sharing. The vehicle would restrict them to the road, dangerously, but also be swift.

Pen disemboweled Prygos's purse to make sure the coach was the smallest and lightest available, the horses a team of four to be managed by a postilion riding one of the front pair, out of earshot. He feigned it would allow him to continue his healing en route, but its overwhelming advantage was the privacy it would give him to open the next stage of his negotiations. Which were going to go somewhere past delicate and through awkward to, possibly, incendiary.

Because by the time they reached Skirose, some one-hundred-eighty miles farther on, he must somehow persuade Arisaydia and Nikys to turn east with him to the coast. There to find some fishing vessel to deliver them to the island of Corfara, and from there, passage to Lodi in Adria. And if he couldn't...

Then we still need to turn east, said Des.

ARISAYDIA REFUSED to be dressed again in his sister's clothes, but did, grudgingly, consent to be muffled in the green cloak and hurried through the inn to the waiting coach. Once inside, and started on their rattling way, he instantly divested it, bundled it up, and thrust it back at Nikys, seated next to him. "You are never to speak of this."

She returned a musical sort of "Mmm!" that promised nothing, and Penric discovered how enchanting her round face grew when she smiled deeply enough to dimple. Thwarted, Arisaydia switched his glower to Pen, more convincingly.

Penric had taken the rear-facing seat across from them, along with their meager baggage. Making sure his feet were firmly planted on the sword scabbard laid on the floor, he tried to evolve a plausible way to open his negotiation. Which must also entail his confession. Arisaydia took the problem out of his hands.

"What did Prygos's clerk—Tepelen, Velka, whoever he was—mean when he said you were supposed to be drowned? He knew you. And you knew him."

Penric cleared his throat. "Ah. Yes. That's something we need to discuss. I'd been putting it off till after I was sure I could restore your sight. That time has come."

Arisaydia made an impatient *so get on with it* gesture.

Penric signed himself, tapped his lips twice with his thumb, and gave a short, seated bow. "Permit me to introduce myself more fully. I am Learned Penric of Martensbridge, formerly court sorcerer to the late princess-archdivine of that canton. For the last year, I've been in service to the archdivine of Adria. Who, for my command of the Cedonian language and certain other skills, loaned me to his cousin the duke, to dispatch as his envoy in response to your letter begging honorable military employment in his realm."

Nikys's eyes widened.

Arisaydia barked, "I wrote no such letter!"

"Forged, yes. Velka confirmed that. It was a plot from the start. Velka, who had been following me in the ship from Lodi, seized the duke's quite authentic reply as soon as I set foot ashore in Patos. Velka knew I was the envoy but didn't know my real name nor, I suspect, my real calling. Although I'm not sure they would have treated me any differently if they had. They cracked my skull and tossed me down a bottle dungeon in the shore fortress. The night after you were blinded, they tried to drown me in my cell. Tying up a loose end, I expect."

Nikys gasped. "How did you escape?"

Penric, who had worked out in his head a scholarly letter on his novel method during his nights in the sickroom, almost opened his mouth to start spouting the preamble, then realized that wasn't really the question being asked. "Magic."

Arisaydia sat back, glaring fiercely. "More likely he was let go. Agent or unwitting cat's-paw, could be either."

Penric, affronted, snapped, "If you must know, when the water was halfway up the cell I turned some of it to ice and stood on it to reach the opening."

"I don't believe that," scoffed Arisaydia. Nikys looked more doubtful.

Penric sighed and sat back. "Just a minute..." He held up his pinched fingers and concentrated. Des had been right in her theory about water in the desert, or at least in Cedonia, he was pleased to see, as the tiny, intense spot of cold grew to a hailstone half an inch across. He leaned forward, pulled out Arisaydia's palm, and dropped the chip into it. Arisaydia, looking vaguely horrified, shook it hastily out of his hand. For good measure, Pen made a bigger one for Nikys; she, at least, rewarded him with a more appropriate look of awe. And, after a moment, bent forward to taste it.

"Don't—!" her brother began, but she crunched it between her teeth and smiled.

"It really is ice! They had ice sometimes at court in Thasalon," she told Penric, "but they brought it down out of the mountains in winter and stored it underground." She narrowed her eyes. "If you are a Temple sorcerer, you must owe final allegiance to the Bastard's Order, yes?"

"He is my chosen god, yes." Or choosing one—Pen had never been quite sure. "I did really attend the white god's seminary at Rosehall, which is associated with the university corporate body there."

"But not its medical faculty?" *You lied?* her eyes asked.

Penric waved this away. "I had enough on my plate then just with the theology, since I was doing everything backward, and in a hurry. A Temple sorcerer is supposed to train as a divine first, and only then be invested with a demon. Everything caught up with itself eventually."

She tilted her head, lips firmed with a different flavor of doubt than her brother's. "You are neither quack nor charlatan. Your skills, even if uncanny, couldn't have come out of the air."

And *there* was a place he didn't wish to dwell. "They were hard-earned, just not all by me. But this is beside the point. I was sent here as a go-between, not as a physician. The duke of Adria was quite sincere in desiring to take you into his train, General Arisaydia, and would be pleased if I were to return with you. And your sister. At present you are running away, but that's not enough; you need to be running toward. If we turn for the coast at Skirose, I think I can get us all aboard a ship for Adria."

"Ship captains don't like to take sorcerers aboard," Arisaydia observed, in a temporizing tone. "They say it's bad luck."

Not nearly as bad of luck as being caught helping an Imperial fugitive, Pen suspected. "Eh, hedge sorcerers, certainly. The Temple-trained know enough not to shed chaos in the rigging, and, further, know how not to."

"Can mariners tell the difference?"

"Generally not, which is another reason why I travel incognito."

Nikys was staring back and forth between them, clearly taken aback by this new proposal to dispose of her life unconsulted. "I don't speak Adriac. I speak a little Darthacan."

Pen smiled hopefully at her. "I could help. I could translate. I could teach you."

By their dual frowns, Pen didn't think he was making much headway. He tried again to bring things back to the issue: "The duke really does want you. He thinks with your skills and experience you'd slice through the forces of Carpagamo like a knife through butter, and I concur. Although even you might break a tooth on their canton mountain mercenaries. Unless the duke hired you some canton troops of your own, I suppose, although that could get very awkward and messy and probably is not a good idea. Certainly not for my poor cantons." He added after a moment, "Adria and Carpagamo do no end of horrible things to one another, as opportunity presents, but at least I can promise you blinding is not public policy there."

It was Nikys who pulled the unravelling thread from this. "You aren't really half Cedonian, are you? That was another lie."

"Ah, no. I'm from the valley of the Greenwell, in the mountains about a hundred miles east of Martensbridge. I don't think you would find it on a Cedonian-made map." Or most other maps, truth to tell.

"Are the cantons even a country?" said Arisaydia in unflattering doubt.

"Mm, more a patchwork of...*city-states* is too grand—call us town-states. Conquerors from the Old Cedonian Empire to Great Audar of Darthaca to Saone and the Weald have all tried to hold various of the cantons, but none have succeeded for long. We have no tolerance for foreign misrule. We prefer our *own* misrule." A little homesick grin twitched Pen's mouth. "Not that there's much profit in conquest. Our mountains have few productive mines, and our fields are worse. Unless you like goats and cows. Our main exports are cheese and mercenaries.

Both quite good," he added in a faint spasm of patriotism. "It snows a lot," he ran down. "When it isn't raining. Perhaps that's why I'm good with ice." Gods, he was tired.

"Mad as three boots," muttered Arisaydia, cryptically.

"Adria," said Pen, "would pay you well."

Arisaydia's mouth twisted in disgust. "No doubt." He raised his chin, his garnet eyes glinting. "I was never in correspondence with the duke of Adria. I was in correspondence with the duke of *Orbas.*"

Pen's eyes widened; Des murmured, *Aha!* Now, *there* was a missing piece fallen into place...

"I'd not got so far as telling him to go jump in the sea, although that was next. A happy interruption, in retrospect. When we arrive at Skirose, you are welcome to go home to Adria, with my best curses. Nikys and I will strike south for Orbas."

He sat back and folded his arms, stony. Nikys's lips parted, and a hand lifted, but fell back, whatever she thought given no voice.

Arisaydia added, "And if you try to lay a geas on me like those bloody horses, I'll run you through."

Surreptitiously, Pen put a little more weight on the scabbard under his foot. "That would be harder for me than it looks. And harder for you than you think."

Arisaydia snorted and closed his eyes, shutting out…everything. Pen could see his point.

XII

A STRAINED, EXHAUSTED SILENCE filled the coach, broken by the bustle of changing the horses at the first fifteen miles. A servant sold them cups of thin ale, which Nikys drank for lack of any better beverage, and they took turns at the livery's privy. She seized a moment when the physician...sorcerer... *Learned* Penric, an oath-sworn Temple divine *ye gods,* was out of earshot to draw Adelis aside beneath a tree overhanging the coach yard.

"It's all very well to spurn the duke of Adria, but have you noticed that Penric is the only one among us with any money?"

"I thought you had some." Adelis, certainly, had been hurried out of the villa with little more than her clothes on his back.

"Enough for a night at an inn and a few meals, maybe. Not enough to get us to Orbas. If that's our destination, the man emptying out his purse to buy us passage all the way to Skirose was a boon." And the continuous travel through the coming night, purchased at a premium, would give them a significant edge on any pursuit.

"I believe that was Secretary Prygos's purse, but yes. Getting it away from the sorcerer could be tricky."

"I wasn't actually suggesting we repay his bounty by robbing the man," Nikys said a little tartly. "He could be an extraordinary resource." The fact that he'd served princesses, archdivines and dukes hinted at a high level of standing that the man himself concealed. "You don't wish to be conscripted by Adria…"

His laugh was short and humorless. "My Adriac is poor, I get sick on ships, and I have no desire to let those sea rats use me against Cedonia, which I don't doubt they'd try to do sooner or later, Carpagamo be hanged. No." He added in a lower tone, as if embarrassed by the hope, "From Orbas, I might have some chance of eventually reinstating myself with Thasalon. From Adria I'd have none."

Nikys considered this. "Something dire would have to happen to Minister Methani and his hangers-on, to allow you that."

Adelis's teeth glinted, feral below the wreck of his face. "Probably."

She took a steadying breath. "So what do you say we turn it around and try to conscript Penric to Orbas?" *Or to ourselves?*

"I'm still trying to figure out how to safely shed him. As I've refused to make myself his duke's man, he has no reason not to betray us."

"I think that's about as likely as an artist setting fire to his master-painting. For all that he mumbles around it, he seems wildly proud of what he's done for your eyes." As well he should be, she suspected. If she hadn't known it was magic, she'd have dubbed it miracle.

"Nikys, he's an Adriac agent. Self-confessed!"

"He's a lot more than that."

Adelis snorted. "Are you sure it's Orbas you desire him for?"

Her lips twitched up; she hoped she wasn't flushing. "It's true I've come to like him. He's just… different. Strange, but not unkind."

"That was a *jest*." Adelis's eyes narrowed in new suspicion. "Has he offered you any offense? He's not been…trying to seduce you in some sorcerous way, has he?"

She had to laugh at this. "I don't think he'd need sorcery for that, but no." *Alas* was probably not the best thing to add.

Adelis being Adelis, he heard it anyway. "Of all the—! I introduced you to any number of honest officers, yet you want to make cow's eyes at some foreign little, little…"

"He's taller than you," Nikys pointed out, as he groped for a word to sum Penric. She thought he'd need an oration at the least.

"Skinny then, twitchy, lying…he has a chaos demon inside him! If he were doing something to you, could you tell? I can't!"

"Then maybe he's not. Wasn't. Whichever." Was that alarm the root of his antipathy? Or was the antipathy his alarm's disguise? She took a breath to tame her temper. "We can certainly both see what he has done *for* you. That ought to give you a comparison." She could grant that the very invisibility of Penric's magic was disturbing—how could a man defend against an attack he could not see? But she didn't usually need to squeeze fair judgment out of Adelis like oil from an olive press. "I'd think Thasalon just gave you a sharp lesson in the hazards of imagining threats where there are none."

He did flinch at that one, and backed down a tiny Adelis-inch, worth a yard from any other man. "I just believe he could be dangerous. To you."

She folded her arms, her head tilting at this blatant hypocrisy. "Then you shouldn't have taught me not to be afraid of dangerous men, hm?"

He knew enough not to step into this quagmire, but he soon found another, saying grumpily, "I'd think you'd be jealous of a fellow who's prettier than you."

"Why, are you? Really, Adelis!" She spotted the man in question emerging around the side of the stable, and had to admit that last fraternal jape was part-right. Not about the jealousy, though, which would be as futile as envying the sunlight. "Hush, here he comes back."

They climbed once more into the close confines of the coach and were off, rumbling and bumping along at a smart, steady trot.

A few miles farther on, they were passed by a galloping provincial courier. Penric glanced out the window and frowned. Minutes later, the horse came cantering back down the track, bucking and kicking at its saddle turned under its belly, followed at length by the panting, swearing courier. Adelis craned his neck to look after them as they fell behind.

"Did you do that?" he asked Penric.

"Yes," he sighed. "I'm not sure it will actually help anything."

Adelis drummed his fingers on the window rim. "I don't like being trapped on this road."

Penric shrugged. "We can count on a one-day start at least. I guarantee Velka won't be recovered enough to ride yet. And then, if he means to pursue me, he'll be put to requisitioning a sorcerer from the Patos Temple, or wherever one might be obtained. If the Temple in Cedonia is anything like the ones I know, the delays will be maddening. Although if they think I'm a hedge sorcerer, they'll take the request seriously. Controlling hedge sorcery is in their mandate regardless of the politics."

"If we could find a coach, so could Velka," said Adelis. "With or without his own pet sorcerer."

"Hm."

"You didn't cripple him permanently." The least Penric might have done, Adelis seemed to imply, even if his status as a learned Temple divine finally explained why he would not kill.

"No."

"Why not?"

"I suppose the simplest answer is...to avoid accumulating theological damage to ourselves?" Penric frowned. "I understand the drift of your questions, Arisaydia. Every realm's army tries to tap the Temple for destructive sorcerers, even as rare as we are. I won't say my superiors never give in, but someone is always sorry later. Generally the sorcerer. It's a known hazard."

Adelis accepted this with a provisional "Hm," of his own. Nikys was increasingly sensible that there was disciplined thought behind what the sorcerer would or would not do, even if the hidden rules of it escaped her. To the point where she was starting to wonder if his claimed age of thirty might be a lie in the *other* direction.

Though there was Desdemona, at two-hundred-and-something. It was deceptively easy, but wrong, to overlook Penric's permanent passenger. And then Nikys wondered what all this looked like from the demon's point of view.

At the third change they downed a hot meal at the tavern associated with the livery, then fitted themselves into the coach for the next stage. It really wasn't possible to keep up the morning's tension when Nikys wanted no part of it and Penric folded himself in a boneless slouch, vaguely amiable once more. When he offered to fill the time with another healing session, Adelis wavered.

"What if I pledge to stick to restoring your eyebrows?" Penric said.

"How can I tell what in the Bastard's hell you're doing anyway?" asked Adelis, though his aversion was plainly flagging.

"What does it feel like?" asked Nikys, curious.

Adelis shrugged and admitted, "Strangely soothing, usually."

"This is going to be a long ride," Nikys pointed out, and Adelis allowed himself to be persuaded.

They switched seats, and the two men worked themselves awkwardly around to give Penric's hands access to Adelis's head. This left rather a lot of sorcerous leg to be disposed of somehow; his feet ended up nearly on Nikys's lap.

At length, Adelis's eyelids drifted closed.

"Is he asleep?" Nikys whispered.

"No," growled Adelis, and the corner of Penric's mouth tweaked up. So, his guard was not so far down as that. But the bonelessness seemed to drain out of Penric and into his patient. Penric, by contrast, seemed to grow tenser and more jittery, his brow sheened with sweat.

At their next change, Penric gave them both a tight smile. "I need to take a turn around the stable. Back in a bit. Don't leave without me, heh."

Nikys, inquisitive, got down and followed after him. The stable was cool and dim, pleasant with the bulks of the horses resting in their stalls, munching rhythmically at their fodder. She saw his lean silhouette pass out the far doors.

She emerged at the manure pile, its acrid aroma saturating the air, where the buzz of flies was dying down. Along with the flies. Penric leaned against the stable wall with his arms folded, watching their devastation somewhat glumly.

"What *are* you doing?"

"The disorder harvested from the healing has to go somewhere, and death makes the most efficient sink of chaos. Killing flies, or fleas, or any other vermin assigned to the Bastard, is theologically allowable sacrifice. Most red-blooded animals are the province of the Son of Autumn, but there are a few exceptions. Rats, mice, other creatures making pests of themselves where they shouldn't be. My god's elder Brother may owe me a favor or two, but I shouldn't like to presume. Thus, flies. Which are tedious but always abundant."

It was possibly the most bizarre conversation she'd had in her life but, oddly, not frightening. She leaned against the wall beside him and folded her arms too, a silent offer of company. He cast her a quick, grateful smile.

"But never people." It was comforting to reflect on that.

His smiled faded. "Well…"

She glanced up, letting her eyes speak her doubt.

"Not quite never. For the Bastard is the god of exceptions, after all, and the son of His Mother. In the highest levels of medical sorcery, there are a few exemptions. Not at all the sort of *him versus me* contests your brother pictures, so don't tell him. He'd get excited and try to make something of it that it isn't. When the choices are one life or another, or one life or none..." He trailed off.

She let her silence stand open, waiting to be filled with whatever he chose. Or didn't. Not for all the world would she press him. It might be like pressing too hard on glass.

"After which the physician gets to spend his nights face down on the temple floor, praying for a sign and receiving silence. Not devotions I'd wish on...anyone."

"I..." Could she honestly say *I see?* She changed it to, "I'm sorry."

The yard before them had fallen deathly still.

He drew breath. "Aye, me too." He shoved off from the wall, his smile carefully reaffixed, and they turned back through the stable.

And what, exactly, did this erratic-seeming, young-seeming man know about *the highest levels of medical sorcery?*

She was beginning to suspect that the answer might be *Everything.*

Which trailed the question, like a net behind a boat, *How?*

⟡

IN THE late afternoon the Patos plains gave way to climbing hill country, and their progress slowed. Nikys's only consolation was the reflection that the rugged slopes would delay pursuers equally. A third pair of horses was hitched to their little coach, at a price, to haul them over the highest pass.

The sorcerer alternated between more healing sessions, growing intense now that his patient seemed soon to be parted from him, and staggering out to shed his chaos however he could at every stop. With her packed so close, and the labors so relentless, Nikys began to see the effects not only on Adelis but on Penric. *He's draining himself.*

Freed at last to talk about his craft, Penric did. He didn't sound much like a spy, but he did sound quite like a frustrated scholar with a favorite subject and a captive audience. She wondered if he was one of those inexplicable people who talked more, not less, as they grew tireder. Adelis was bestirred to open curiosity at last, despite his reservations, although his probing questions tended to revolve around military applications.

No, no one could muster a troop of sorcerers. Demons did not well tolerate each other, which was also why one only heard of a single court sorcerer at a time. No, one sorcerer did not differ greatly from another in raw power; all were limited by the amount of chaos a human body could safely hold and shed at a time. The differences in skill were mainly due to cleverness and efficiency, which age and experience enhanced. The inefficient working of magic generated, among other things, heat; a clumsy sorcerer might pass out from the heat or (a vile grin) perhaps burst like a grilled sausage, who knew? Nikys wasn't sure she believed that one, nor, from the look on his face, did Adelis. If the latter were true, Penric temporized, no one had lived to report on it, so proof was hard to come by.

No (a wistful sigh), no sorcerer could shoot fire-balls from his or her fingertips. The two men looked equally disappointed at this. "Although I'm a pretty fair hand at shooting flaming arrows," Penric added. "But that's archery, not sorcery."

No, no, no, and through repeated discouragement Penric gently led Adelis away from hypothetical military schemes involving sorcery, or at least this sorcerer.

Nikys wondered how all this negative certainty sat with the god of exceptions and exemptions. Slippery as a fish, indeed.

Her own questions seemed to fall on more fertile ground. Yes, physician-sorcerers were rare. Only the tamest and most domesticated of Temple demons, cultivated over several demon-lives, or rather, the lives of their learned riders, were considered suitable and safe to be paired with an already-trained and skilled physician. Yes, two hundred years was unusually old for any demon. Most new elementals did not last so long in the world, being hurried out of it by a saint of the Bastard's Order dedicated to the task, or some other accident. The longer a demon survived, the more likely it was to seize ascendance in its rider's body, and without its rider's disciplines its fundamental chaos would come to the fore, to disaster all around. Yes, demons took the imprints of their personalities from their human partners, for good or ill. Given some humans, this could turn out very ill indeed, making it quite unfair that it was the *demon* who suffered instantaneous sundering and utter destruction when its god caught up with it at last.

Nikys wasn't sure if this last gloss came from Penric or Desdemona, though it was delivered quite fiercely.

As night fell in the rocking coach even the chatty Penric ran down to miserable endurance. Adelis put on his campaign face and went stolid. Nikys drooped.

She and Adelis took turns leaning on each other, napping badly. Penric folded himself this way and that in his seat, each position looking more uncomfortable than the last, finally lifting his legs to prop near the roof, more-or-less bracing himself in place.

She might have brought more comforts if this flight had been planned, conducted in suitable secrecy, instead of forced pell-mell, with pursuit pelting hot. *If wishes were horses, we all would ride,* the old nursery saw went, and remounts were another thing she was going to be wishing hard for when they reached Skirose.

Where they would be running out of time, money, stamina…everything.

❦

THEY CAME to Skirose at the next day's dusk. Stumbling out of the coach at last, Nikys wondered if Penric had felt anything like this escaping the bottle dungeon. At a cheaper, grubbier inn they found only one room to share, but it offered water to wash with and a flat, unmoving bed to fall into. The innkeeper dragged in a thin, wool-stuffed pallet to lay on the floor. Penric grimaced and casually rid it of crawling, biting wildlife, for good measure passing his hand over the bed. She and Adelis took the bed and Penric took the pallet. Her head was swimming, Penric's blue eyes were clouded with fatigue, and Adelis's stolidity was ossifying. Danger or no, a few hours of sleep could no longer be put off.

Deep in the night she awoke to see Penric, who like all of them had lain down half dressed, pull on his jacket and slip out through the shadows. Adelis was snoring. Was the sorcerer making his escape to Adria? Planning some final, belated betrayal? Alarmed, she slid into her shoes, whipped her cloak around her, and followed him on tiptoe.

He exited silently through the inn's front door; she waited a moment and did the same, flattening to the wall and looking around for that narrow form, without torch or lantern, flickering in and out of the moonlight. She pulled up her hood and tracked him down the street and around a corner. He crossed a

paved square and disappeared under a temple portico. She waited for the second creak of a heavy
door, then dared to run to catch up. What did he
want inside?

He'd left the door ajar; she eased it open with
no betraying sound, and found a deeper shadow to
stand in. The moon, just past full, shone directly
down into the sacred atrium, pulling short the blue
shadow of the fire plinth. A few red coals gleamed
in its ashes. As her eyes adjusted, she spotted Penric
making his slow way around the perimeter from
altar to altar, signing himself, then cursorily opening what she'd thought were supposed to be locked
offering boxes and helping himself to the contents,
tipping the coins into his purse. Which did explain
how he'd been finding funds since his escape from
the bottle dungeon, apart from pickpocketing provincial officials. He skipped the Mother's offering
box, although he signed himself and bowed his
head before Her place all the same.

At the Bastard's offering box, he murmured,
"Hm. They must love You better in these hills." He
topped off his purse, but, instead of merely bowing,
went down on his knees before the altar with its
white cloth. He raised his hands palms-out in an

attitude of supplication; after a minute, he instead lay prone on the tiles, arms out in the attitude of deepest supplication. Or possibly exhaustion.

Quiet fell. Yet not, she thought, quietude, for in a minute he mumbled, "Who am I fooling, kindest-and-cruelest Sir? You never answer me anyway."

His voice went acerbic. "Fool indeed, to invite His attention. This is not something we want. Really."

Nikys had no wish to interrupt a prayer, but this seemed more like an argument. She walked over and sat herself down cross-legged beside the…physician, sorcerer, divine? Which of his bewildering multiplicity of selves had laid itself down in such hope-starved humility?

He rolled over on his back and smiled at her, seeming unsurprised. "Hullo, Nikys. Come to pray?"

"Maybe."

He bent his head back toward the white-topped altar. "Is this your god too? I think you said so, once back in Patos."

"For lack of answers to my prayers from any others, yes."

"My condolences."

She wasn't sure how to take that. "I've been wanting to tell you. I had another idea, back in the coach."

"Oh?"

"Instead of Adelis going to Adria with you, which he will not, why don't you come to Orbas with us?"

The little noise he made was altogether uninformative, although it sounded vaguely like a man being hit. Then he paused, doubtful. "Does Arisaydia endorse this?"

"I'm sure I could talk him around," said Nikys, a little airily. "Once we are established there, Adelis could help you to some honorable appointment. Maybe even court sorcerer."

"Likely the duke already has one. That's how I lost my last position, you know. When Princess-Archdivine Llewen died so suddenly, the replacement archdivine brought her own trusted sorceress from Easthome. I offered to stay quietly apart among my books and papers—I wasn't even done with my latest translation—but no one seemed to think there was room in the palace for two chaos demons. Not even the chaos demons."

Wait, was that last delivered in his other voice? But he was going on, speaking his reminiscence to the night sky framed by the inner architrave.

"They all tried their hardest to shift me into the Martensbridge Mother's Order, which wanted me as much as the Palace suddenly did not. Very tidy. Everyone happy but me. No man should have to bury two mothers in one year."

Her neck felt wrenched with this last turn. "What?"

He waved a hand, dismissing she-knew-not-what. "Princess Llewen had been like a second mother to me. My own mother's death happened not long after, back at Jurald Court. I wasn't there for either one. Not sure if that was a blessing or a curse."

"I'm sorry." Surely more inadequate words were never spoken, but his hand waved again, this time in understanding acceptance. She tried to find her way back to her proposal. "If not court sorcerer, Orbas must surely be willing to make you court physician." Eager, once they learned what he'd done for Adelis.

Without heat, and with some precision, Penric said, "I would rather die." His smile grew small and strange.

Nikys sat up, gathering her determination. "I've been trying to work out why a man of your obvi-ous—extraordinary—skills would not take up the healing trade. I think I know."

"Do you? Tell me." His tone was ironic, but not malicious. There didn't seem to be a malicious bone in his body.

"You lost a patient. Maybe someone important to you"—could it have been his princess? his mother?—"maybe just someone you tried too hard for, and it broke your heart, and your will to go on." She tried to gauge his reaction out of the corner of her eye. Was she too bold, too offensive? Would he be angry at her probing?

She hadn't expected to evoke a crack of laughter, cut off sharp, and she flinched. *Mad as a boot*, Adelis had said. Was the observation shrewder than she'd guessed?

"If only that." Penric stretched back on the temple floor, folded his hands behind his head, and squinted up at the moon, which bathed his pale face in pale light until he looked carved of snow. "Try three a week. More, some weeks."

"What?"

"This is a place for confessions, why not? After tomorrow we are unlikely to see each other again, even better. Like lancing an infection, and as ugly yet fascinating as what drains from one, aye. Might be good for me."

Three boots? She bit her lip.

"Everything started well. I was happy in my scholar's work for the princess-archdivine. But due to my transcription and translations of Learned Ruchia's germinal volumes on sorcery and medicine, the Mother's Order at Martensbridge found out that two of Desdemona's former riders had been physicians. The princess was eager to add another string to my bow, and so was I, when she sent me over to their hospice to learn. Apprentice, we all thought, until all of Learned Amberein's and Learned Helvia's knowledge began to awaken in me, and suddenly I was doing as much teaching as learning. Not that every new patient isn't a lesson for every physician, lifelong. I did enjoy instructing the apprentices in anatomy.

"I brought off some difficult cures. It all depends, you know, on underlying conditions. If they'd taken your brother's eyes with hot irons, it would have left me too little to work with. But from the outside, no one could tell why I sometimes succeeded and sometimes failed.

"The hospice began to ask more and more of me because, after all, it *sometimes* worked. Worth trying, you know? I was stretched, but still holding my own, when the princess passed away and I lost a defender I didn't realize I'd had.

"You see, the Order's idea of conserving me was to save me for only the worst cases. I never got to treat, I don't know, a hangnail, or even worms anymore, I never was allowed any *easy* victories. Always and only the direst injuries and illnesses, over and over. Far more died than not. When I found myself walking to the hospice each day devising…well, it doesn't matter now."

"It matters to me," Nikys dared.

His moon-silvered brows flicked up. "Whyever? Whatever. I did promise a full confession, didn't I. As I sit—lie down—speak before my god. Not that He doesn't already know." A snow-smile, barely bending. "So, when I spent my walk to work each day thinking up methods for a sorcerer to kill himself—which is not an easy thing to do, it turns out, when his demon opposes the idea—I realized perhaps it might be time to stop. I made application to the archdivine of Adria for work in translation, and other Temple scholarship, and ended my career as sorcerer-physician in Martensbridge. It was good, traveling north over the mountains. It felt like a narrow escape."

Nikys tried for a friendly silence. Because the alternative was to cry out in horror and protest, and that would certainly not be helpful. Just how far had that *devising* gone? *I'd bet Desdemona could tell me.*

Penric continued, "And thus I learned the difference between a skill and a calling. To have a calling with no skill is a tragedy anyone can understand. The other way around…less so."

"Oh. I…see." She took a breath and cast her own challenge. "You know, I should really like to hear Desdemona's version of this."

She'd startled him; his eyes went wide. In an uncertain voice he said, "I suppose…we could do that."

She could catch, now, when that inner twin shifted the tensions in his face. The demon spoke: "Hah. *We* blame his superiors entirely. Amberein and Helvia both trained up in the greatest centers of the medical arts in Saone and Darthaca, in their days, where their skills and limits were properly understood, together with the reticence needed to sustain them. Backwards Martensbridge saw only that a magical boon had fallen to them, and wanted to milk it for all it could give. Like a greedy trainer putting a high-blooded colt to race too soon, to its ruin. And Penric, the fool, wouldn't say no and wouldn't quit, till we both ended up on a hillside at dawn seeing if I could heal his arms faster than he could slice them open, which was *not* my idea of how we should part ways."

"It wasn't *serious*." His voice shifted to a tone of dissent. "There was a precipice near enough if I'd been serious. As you have several times pointed out, you can't make us fly."

"Fortunately, he passed out before he could win the contest. A small landslide and an unlucky elk paid for the rest, and when he woke up, we had a *talk*."

Penric may have been confessing; this sounded more like ranting.

"And he *still* won't say no and he won't quit, which is how we ended up in a bottle dungeon in Patos instead of a nice, comfortable study in Lodi overlooking the canal. What he *needs* is a superior with the backbone to say *no* for him." His voice went sly, and his eyes shifted toward her. "A woman with experience keeping fool men alive might do the trick."

"Des!" He convulsed to a sitting position.

"What, you're the one who's been mooning after her hips for the past fortnight. So do something about it."

His jaw snapped shut. In this light, it was impossible to tell if he blushed, but his cheeks darkened a little.

Nikys gulped, not doubting she'd caught the demon's drift. Though not the first, it certainly ranked as the strangest proposition she'd ever received. Also, curiously, the least insulting. "Experience I have," she said quietly. "Success, very little."

"Worth asking," came the mutter, and she wasn't sure which of the people in his head said it.

His spine straightened. "It *is* worth asking." Now his voice was his own. He turned his head toward her, eyes silver in the shadows, and unreadable. "I have a counter-proposal for you. What if you came to Adria with me? Let Adelis make his own way to Orbas, which I think he now might do."

She rocked back. "I couldn't do that, I couldn't leave…"

"He left you, to go off to his wars how many times? He might even travel more safely alone, and certainly faster."

"Your duke doesn't want *me*." Her heart was thumping, uselessly.

"I didn't say it was for the duke." He'd gone a little breathless.

"It would make me a hostage against Adelis."

His lips parted, closed. His voice went small. "Wasn't what I had in mind."

"But it would follow. Inevitably. Things being as they are."

"Oh?" He slumped back supine on the floor again, staring up at the advancing moon. "I might protect..."

"When one's own liege-lords turn on one, we have all lately seen how hard *protection* is to come by."

"I suppose that's so."

His was the cruelest kind offer she'd ever received, hopelessly misaimed, like pressing gloves on a handless thief, or flowers on a starving woman. She returned the favor. "There's still Orbas."

His face jerked away, as if dodging a dart. "All my books are back in Adria. I hope."

"Beloved hostages?"

"After a fashion. Which says something sad about me, I'm sure."

She considered this oblique evasion. "There are books in Orbas. The duke has a fine library, I've heard. Books you haven't read. Maybe some you've never heard of." He had not, she recollected, said *No* to Orbas, not in the unyielding way Adelis had refused Adria. Even slippery fish jumped into nets sometimes...

His mouth curled up. "Wisdom bird. Madame Owl. Your brother dubbed you aright."

Yes, and what if Adelis woke up and found them both gone? "We should get back. If you are done here."

He looked pensively around. "No one talking here but us, so I would seem to be." He clambered colt-like to his feet, and offered her a hand to heave herself up.

XIII

$\mathcal{P}$ENRIC TOOK NIKYS'S…Madame Khatai's arm in escort as they walked back through the shadows to the inn. He suppressed a wince at the thought of her having trailed him to the temple alone this late at night, in a strange town.

It was no great distance, observed Des.

Des, just don't…embarrass me with this woman.

Rather do it yourself, would you? An impression of a huff. *If I have to listen to you pine after her, so can she. And rather more usefully.*

It was bad enough that he'd made Nikys listen to his fractured confession. *There are impediments. Starting with my Temple oath to the archdivine of Adria.*

*Your god is the same everywhere, Adria, Cedonia…
or Orbas.*

*My god was just now silent on the subject of my
direction, you will note. As ever. And everywhere. A
sameness of sorts, I suppose.*

*What, you prayed for guidance and in the very
next moment that nice child came and sat down
beside you. I thought she was going to pat you on
the head. I could have told her a board would work
better. What do you expect from Him, a letter
signed and sealed and hand-delivered? A parade
with trumpets?*

Penric said hesitantly, *You like her? You don't
always like the women I, er, meet.*

*They don't always like me. But she seems willing to
learn. Not so sure about the brother.*

*I thought you all found him quite scenic to look
upon.*

Yes, till he opened his mouth and was so rude to us.

*We've met worse. I thought him teachable. Give
him time.*

*The time you aren't planning to allow?
Contradictory, Pen.*

He smiled tightly. *If consistency is what you want,
I've taken oath to the wrong god.*

They made their way as quietly as possible through the inn's front door, Penric turning the key again behind them. The place afforded no night-porter, fortunately. They creaked up the dark stairs and made their way to their chamber, marked by a faint orange glow under the door. He was therefore not too surprised to enter after Nikys and find Arisaydia sitting up in the room's one chair, glaring at them by the light of a tallow candle, his eyes red sparks. His unsheathed sword lay across his lap.

He kept his voice low, but fierce. "Where have you been?"

It must have been alarming for him to wake up to the empty room. Or at least to the absence of his sister; Pen hadn't planned on that. Good that he hadn't gone charging out into the town in some wrong direction and repaid them the jolt. "The temple," he answered, equally quietly.

"At this time of night?"

"The gods will hear prayers any time."

"Actually," said Nikys, doffing her cloak and hanging it on a peg, "I found him robbing the offering boxes."

At Arisaydia's stare, Penric said, "You want to hire horses tomorrow, don't you?"

"I was afraid we would be pressed to forage for mounts like an army in enemy territory," he admitted reluctantly. "But buying would be better still, to leave no witnesses to our direction."

"You were thinking of stealing them?" said Nikys, her brows rising. She glanced sidelong at Pen. "It's hard to imagine Cedonia as an enemy country."

Arisaydia's hand touched his temple, as if to say, *Not so hard for me now.* But he clearly still mourned this hostile transformation, even as he set his face to the wind. "No horses for sale in this crossroads village at this time of night anyway." He sighed out his tension and rose. "Try to sleep."

At least he sheathed his sword before he lay down again, but he did pass Penric a special brotherly glower as he blew out the candle.

Pen lay on his pallet and sorted out his options.

There weren't that many. From Skirose, a lesser military road ran east to the sea, and west over the spine of Cedonia to link up with the net of roads around Thasalon. A minor local road ran south into the hills, branching into tracks unfit for wheeled vehicles over the stony passes to the neighboring province. It was another hundred or so miles across that province to the next range of mountains. Beyond them lay the lands of Orbas, Cedonia's sometimes-client-state, sometimes-ally, sometimes-enemy, presently attempting a neutral independence. Thasalon would be happy to forcibly reconvert it to a tax-paying province, if the emperor didn't have a compass-turn of other pressures to attend to: Adria to the east, the Roknari to the north coast and islands, the Rusylli to the southwest.

Penric's most direct route home was east to the sea and across it to Adria. Overland, it would be a longer journey, south around the arc of the coast through Orbas and Trigonie, before he came to Adriac lands once more. Although once to Orbas, he would no longer be running as an outlaw of sorts, and could presumably report to the Temple and seek aid from a local chapter of the Bastard's Order. So heading south with Arisaydia and his sister—all right, with Nikys and her brother—wouldn't be *deciding* anything, necessarily. An alternate course would be to find a coastal ship to take them to one of the few ports of Orbas, although Pen doubted his ability to persuade Arisaydia aboard a form of transport he could neither control nor abandon at will.

Nikys would, of course, follow her twin. Not some possibly-lunatic stranger she'd just met a fortnight ago. Arisaydia was correct, if not right, to take that for granted. Did he realize how much he assumed of her?

Not that oh-so-Learned Penric was in a position to offer her anything better than a different dangerous flight and uncertain welcome, now was he?

Pen, said Des, exasperated, *what you are in a position to do is to stop fretting and go to* sleep, *so we aren't all worthless for* any *action in the morning.*

She wasn't wrong. He grumbled and rolled over.

⌘

THEY ATE breakfast soon after dawn in the inn's common room, as apart from its other patrons as they could arrange, and silently. Fare included porridge, unexceptional, dried figs and apricots, decent, a small ration of white cheese, horrifyingly familiar squares of dried fish which Nikys and Arisaydia consumed without comment, and an excessively generous bowl of tough half-dried black olives, which Penric sampled suspiciously and passed along to his companions. After, they returned to their room to count out Pen's coins on the washstand, and plan.

"If we make for the coast," Pen reasoned, "and then pick up passage on some local vessel, we could as soon reach the ports of Orbas as the island of Corfara. Which must surely be easier on Madame Khatai than an overland flight through these hills." And it would give Penric several more days to argue for Adria, if he could evolve some better lever to shift this human boulder. A frown from Nikys indicated that this slight on her endurance was not entirely appreciated, but an appeal to Arisaydia's own convalescent state would have been worse received.

Arisaydia appeared not totally unmoved by the argument, or at least his scowl grew more thoughtful. He glanced at Nikys and seemed to consider. "Our funds might purchase one maybe-sound horse. Not three," he said at last. "Give the purse to Nikys, and we'll go dicker for hired horses. You go and buy us food to last for a two-day ride. We'll meet back here and decide on our direction then."

It wasn't a *yes*, but it wasn't as firm a *no* as usual. Penric elected not to push, or push his luck, just yet, and went off to find whatever passed for a day-market in this town. And marshal his next set of points. Debate had never been his best skill, back in seminary.

He returned with a sack of variously preserved foods, including more leathery olives, and settled on a bench in the inn's entry atrium, tilting his straw hat down over his face, to await the siblings' return with horses.

And waited.

Growing restless, he went up to check their chamber. No notes. Arisaydia and Nikys had taken their scant belongings with them to pack in the hoped-for saddlebags, and Pen's case stood ready to go. Arisaydia was not a man to waste time.

Indeed, not.

A weight settled in Pen's stomach that had nothing to do with porridge and olives, and he hastened downstairs and around to the main street that hosted the livery and coaching inn serving the military road. A quick survey of the ostlers came up only with no, no sir, a man and a woman had not tried to hire three riding horses in the last couple of hours, nor even two horses. Was there any other livery in town? Oh, aye, sir, there was a little place just off the west road, but it only offered local hires, not good coach teams like ours, twelve miles an hour on the flats! Reflecting that this country was not oversupplied with flats,

Penric lengthened his stride as he found his way to the west road.

The stable on the west road was small but tidy, featuring a dozen stalls, mostly empty. Oh, aye, sir; a man and his wife had hired two horses, together with the requisite groom-guide, and left upwards of two hours gone. Which way? The south road. Something about visiting relatives in a village up the far head of the valleys.

Arisaydia, you son of a bitch, Penric swore, internally. For the stable owner he managed a thin smile. What was left in Pen's pockets wouldn't hire a pony for a ride up and down the street.

He waited till he was out of earshot, stamping back up the road, to curse aloud. It didn't relieve his feelings much. The blasted man hadn't won wars, Pen supposed, by sitting around waiting for the battle to be brought to him. He should have remembered that.

He was smooth, agreed Des, unhelpfully. *If he'd demanded that purse for his own hands, you wouldn't have been near so quick to hand it across.*

Pen growled.

And had Nikys agreed, or argued and been overridden? Gone along eagerly, or regretfully? Pen supposed the clench to his heart made no practical difference either way.

Returning to the inn, Pen cleared his case and sack from a room he could no longer afford, and tried to come up with his next scheme. Walking after his quarry in an attempt to overtake them would be futile. More futile, he suspected, would be catching them. Horse theft, even if a temporary borrowing, would be tricky. *Not impossible, though.* But if that was his plan, he needed to carry it out quickly.

He'd have to wait for nightfall to revisit the moneylenders of the gods in the temple, although raiding the same place twice in a row seemed imprudent. If anyone had noticed the sudden shortfall, they might set a watch tonight. Alternatively, he could give up and start walking to the coast. His worn Cedonian sandals were not his idea of marching gear, but he could replace them at the next town. Where there would be another temple, likely, although perhaps more impoverished. He gnawed a piece of dried fruit from his sack, and fumed.

Mulling feasibility, he hoisted his case and sack and returned to the first livery. It harbored more horses to choose from, but also more people about. Sneaking an animal out in broad daylight would certainly pose a challenge, even for a sorcerer. Waiting for the cover of darkness would be pointless, if the entire purpose was to catch Arisaydia and Nikys. If he were going east afoot, better to start now.

He stood concealed across the street in a niche between two whitewashed houses and, slowly, tore his own hopes in half. He'd done all he could. East it was.

A pair of coaches rolled up, noisy and dusty, each pulled by a lathered team of six. Someone had been paying for speed, to be sure. The ostlers and servants, interpreting the signs of impending largess, swarmed out to take charge. About to step forward, Pen instead jerked back, as the vehicles disgorged a troop of ten soldiers and a sergeant, a man in the loose white robes of the Bastard's Order in Cedonia, and the all-too-familiar figure of Velka.

Heart hammering, Pen scrambled up the side of the house, fingers and toes scraping raw on stonework and sills, to take a concealed vantage on the flat roof, peering down into the street and a bit of the inn yard. Of *course* coaches. If Velka had tried to march a troop after Arisaydia, they wouldn't be more than forty miles from Patos by now.

After some milling about and a rush on the livery's privy, and the successful sale of some tankards of ale swiftly quaffed, the sergeant rounded up his men, counted them off, and sent them spreading out in pairs through the town. "You know what questions to ask by now," he shouted after them. Penric bet he knew, too. *Bastard's teeth.*

Velka, who bore a thin white bandage around his brow, was stiff and limping. It might be the lingering effects of Pen's rough treatment of him three days ago at the villa, but the gray-bearded man in the rumpled whites moved almost as stiffly, so maybe it was just the coach. The glint of silver from the man's shoulder braid would have told Pen what he needed to know even without Desdemona's tight, *Well, Pen. We have a colleague.*

Can you tell anything more without revealing yourself?

Not yet.

Velka began interrogating the ostlers and servants, who answered readily, pointing in various directions. A handing-out of coins reduced the directions by maybe half. Penric wanted to thump his own head—their memory of his recent queries must send Velka on to the other livery much sooner than he would have found it otherwise. Although he would certainly have arrived there in due course. Arisaydia and Nikys couldn't be more than ten miles up the track by now. Maybe there were a lot of possible side trails? Penric hoped for dozens.

It would take Velka some time to collect intelligence, decide on a course, hire or conscript thirteen riding horses. Though the sergeant was already bargaining with the inn servants to get his men a hasty meal, which might well be accomplished while horses were found and saddled. Their demands would strip this stable of mounts, apart from the dozen spent coach horses, useless to Pen. The Temple sorcerer passed within, perhaps looking to his own sustenance.

Velka would shortly know that Pen had been seen separately from Nikys and Arisaydia, and more recently. Pen wondered briefly if he should show himself to get them to chase after him instead? They could well catch him, he recognized ruefully, although they would soon regret doing so. But Velka had enough soldiers to split his forces if he were forced to. He only needed the sorcerer and a couple of men to go after Pen. The rest could ride south, unsparing of their mounts.

Arisaydia would fight to the death before allowing himself to be captured again, Pen suspected, and where would that leave Nikys? Fallen into the hands of some remnant of enraged men, out for revenge for their dead and wounded? Unless the twins should decide to travel together one last time. It seemed a horribly plausible nightmare either way.

Pen swallowed, swung back down the side of the building, collected his case and sack, and slipped through to the next street, not that Skirose had many streets to choose from. He loped west, parallel to but out of sight from the military road. Sneaking up opposite the small livery through someone's scanty grove of olive trees, he spotted two of Velka's men coming back already, marching double-time with their news.

He swore under his breath, waited until they'd angled out of sight, and darted across the road to the stable.

The stable boy rose in far too much alarm to be greeting a potential customer. Pen made one futile attempt to motion him to hush, then, as he turned, yelling and starting to run, tweaked the nerves in his legs and, as soon as possible, his throat. The lad recoiled in terror as Pen rolled him to the side of the aisle, whispering, "Sorry—sorry! It will wear off in a bit." He hoped. He hadn't as much time to prepare his strike as with the soldiers in the villa.

Only one horse was left, a rangy bay gelding turning restlessly in a box stall. *Looks good*, said Des. *Its legs are even longer than yours.*

It also had a spine like a sawblade; ten minutes of bareback trotting would slice a rider up the fork. Pen searched feverishly for a saddle and bridle, and saddlebags, into which he stuffed his case and sack. Back in the stall, he discovered the reason for the beast's lonely state was that it was a biter. And a kicker. And generally uncooperative. At its second yellow-teethed snap, Des gave it a good sting on the nose, mysterious to it since the human it was trying to savage hadn't touched it, and again at the third. It stopped trying after that.

Fitting the bit into its mouth involved ear-wrestling and a near-loss of valuable sorcerous fingers. Pen rechecked the girth—aye, it was a blower, too— and prudently mounted while still in the stall. He let Des undo the latch and swing open the door, and concentrated on keeping the animal's head up on a short rein, and his head down instead of smacked into the door lintel, as it pronked out into the light of the afternoon.

He fought it out onto the road, where it was at least pleased to convert vertical into horizontal motion. Only a sketchy illusion of wolves, a fragment of geas learned from his shaman friend, allowed Pen to force the turn—more of a shy—onto the south road. At that point, he could crouch in his stirrups and let the blighted beast run itself out of piss and vinegar.

It took five miles. Pen, gasping for breath, was impressed. *Bastard's blessing, are you?*

The gallop fell to a bounding trot almost as hard to sit, then a blowing walk. The road followed the winding valley as it rose toward the hill passes. Between patches of tangled woodland, little farmsteads clung to the creek. At one, a woman was out working in a vegetable garden, and Pen dared to stop and beg a drink of water and word of any prior passers-by. She scowled at him in alarm but then, at her second glance, smiled unwilled. The water was forthcoming, but no news; she'd been working inside earlier. Pen cast her a blessing, which made her blink, but then wave back.

He watered the horse when the creek crossed the road, after an argument about whether it was going to try to flop down and roll him off among the rocks. He was only sorry he couldn't give it to Arisaydia. The two deserved each other.

XIV

ADELIS, NIKYS THOUGHT, was champing at the bit far more than their sluggish horses. Pressing their guide for more speed had only won them grudging brisk trots. He was excessively tender toward his employer's beasts, she thought, till they arrived well-timed to stop at what proved a cousin's farmhouse, and an offer of a purchased meal. Adelis whispered, in a furious undervoice more than half serious, that it would be faster to run the man through and steal his horses after all, but yielded to a chance for food that they *only did not have* thanks to leaving Master—Learned—whatever-he-was Penric behind.

The broad, smiling cousin set them out a lunch at a shady table by the stream, in what would have been an idyllic setting and interlude under any other circumstances. As it was, it gave Nikys her first private chance to pick up their argument from back at the livery.

"I still think we were wrong to leave Learned Penric behind. If not tactically, although that too, morally. What if something happens to him?"

Adelis made an exasperated noise through his chewing. "He's a sorcerer. And a spy. He'll land on his feet. Like a cat."

"That's not actually true of cats." Or sorcerers? "And last time, he landed in a bottle dungeon."

"If it's true he was tossed into one, it's also true he escaped. Which is...let's just say unprecedented. He can make his way back to Adria faster and safer without us. That he's an Adriac agent is the one part of his jumble of tales that I certainly believe to be real."

Nikys swallowed watered wine and drummed her fingers on the boards. "I watched him, and talked to him a little, during those first days when you were too lost in pain and syrup of poppies to track much. Whatever else was going through his mind, he cared passionately about what he was try-ing to do for your eyes."

"Which says only that the man had a conscience, which I will not argue about, and that it was guilty. Whether because what he told us was true, or for some other secret up his sleeve, I can't guess. That he was still trying to the last to persuade me to Adria, after all our disasters, that he expended such heroic effort on healing me, suggests that his duke must want me far more than seems reasonable, and I have to wonder why. Nikys, we had only his word for his whole fantastical story. He only claimed to be a Temple sorcerer, and all the rest. We don't know."

"All his actions so far were not proof enough for you?"

Adelis shook his head. "I swear, you swallowed down everything the man said without choking because, what, you liked his blue eyes?"

"You don't deny he's a sorcerer, you can't deny he's an extraordinary physician—what he told me in the temple last night—"

"*He* told," Adelis put in. "Again."

She waved this off. "Well, that was in confidence anyway. As for the other...he thinks better of people than he should. Better than is safe for him. That says more learned divine than spy to me. He thinks differently."

"He and his invisible twelve-headed demon, yes, very differently." A wry grimace as he leaned back.

She still boggled trying to imagine what must be going on inside Learned Penric's overcrowded head. All the time. Whatever else was happening, his mind had to be very, very full. The wonder was not that he was mad but that he wasn't.

"Anyway, we can move faster now," said Adelis.

"Not at present," Nikys noted.

"Aye." He shoved the rest of his bread in his mouth and rose, still chewing. "I'll go prod that groom. And see if I can secure a water bottle. And some food. We'll want them, going over these hills." He went off into the old stone farmhouse.

Nikys thought her greatest want was going to be human, and demonic. Would she ever see the strange sorcerer again? Would he really be all right, as Adelis insisted? His last time—first time, she also gathered—wandering about Cedonia on his own had included some horrifying turns. She hadn't felt this sick with helpless worry since, well, Kymis. And then Adelis, until Penric had appeared. And now

Penric. Her chain of alarming men was getting longer, but no better.

Would there ever be any way to find out if he'd made it home safely? She didn't know a soul in Lodi, had barely met a few Adriac merchants. She supposed one such might carry a letter, but to whom?

But wait, Learned Penric was a Temple-man. If he truly was all he'd said, an inquiry sent in care of the archdivine of Adria might well find him. The ill-fates of recent letters to and from Adria were daunting, but should she and Adelis arrive safely at last in Orbas, she abruptly determined to dare.

There, a plan. Better than crying limply under a persimmon tree any day. As Adelis emerged from the farmhouse, more-or-less strong-arming the groom, she rubbed her eyes and hurried to the horses.

XV

AS THE LIGHT leveled toward evening, the woods dwindled to scrub, the farmsteads gave way to shepherd's huts, and the road narrowed to a winding, stony track. At a bend, Pen encountered a rider leading two saddled horses back the other way.

The rider stopped to stare in surprise. "Five gods, man, someone rented you Pighead? And you're still atop?"

That alone was enough to identify the man as the small livery's groom-and-guide. "Is that its name? Very fitting. We've had some debates along the way, but I've won so far. Tell me, were you escorting a man and his wife, traveling? Where did they go?"

"Oh, aye. I told them they'd never get over the pass before nightfall, better to find shelter and continue in the morning, but they were having none of my advice, so I suppose they deserve what they find. I took them as far up as the horses could get, where they insisted I leave them off."

Pen was still on the right track, five gods be praised. "How much farther? I need to catch up to them."

"Maybe a mile?"

Pen nodded relieved thanks. "Oh, I should warn you—there's a troop of soldiers behind me that are conscripting horses for the army. If you don't want to end up walking home, you'd probably best get your beasts off the road and find a place to hide them till they pass on."

"Oh!" The man looked startled, but he swallowed down the lie. "Thanks!"

"Ah..." Pen's conscience prodded him. If he could only ride a little farther anyway... "Do you want this one, to take back as well?"

The groom grinned. "Naw. Let the army enjoy him."

They each hastened on, in opposite directions.

Indeed, after about a mile of scrambling over slippery scree, footing more suitable to a donkey than to a tired, nervy horse, the trail gave way to outright climbs over stair-like stones, narrowing to a scrubby defile. To Pen's relief, he saw a flash of movement above: a pair of figures, one in a green cloak.

To his dismay, as he turned to look back down the valley before dismounting, he could just make out a troop of mounted soldiers, trotting relentlessly single file. He counted—yes, the whole thirteen. A flicker of white confirmed that Velka had brought his sorcerer. Pen sucked breath through his teeth. The horse, its head hanging in weariness, made one last halfhearted attempt to bite him as he dragged out his belongings from the saddlebags, unbridled it, and turned it loose.

He hoisted his burdens and began clambering up the slope. In a few minutes, Nikys glanced back, spotted him, and touched her brother's sleeve. After a brief debate, they sat on boulders to await his arrival. They both looked nearly spent, but equally determined. Arisaydia still had the sword, naturally.

Penric heaved his way up to them, brandishing the sack. "You forgot your food," he wheezed. "Among other things."

Arisaydia glowered, but Nikys looked tentatively delighted, saying, "After Adelis—after we left you in Skirose, we thought you would certainly go back to Adria. You decided to join with us after all?"

Her smile at him, Pen decided, made up for that vile horse, if not quite for her brother. Not much question whose idea Pen's abandonment had been. "Not exactly. But Velka and a troop arrived in town barely an hour after you'd left. By coach, just as you predicted." He allowed Arisaydia a conceding nod, not received with any discernable gratitude. "They're only a few miles behind us right now."

Nikys's breath drew in. Arisaydia's expression turned a much cooler shade of grim.

By silent, mutual consent, they shelved their differences for later in the face of this news. Arisaydia surveyed the landscape, ending by looking up toward the narrowing defile. "Then we keep climbing. There might be a cave."

"To hide in? He brought his own sorcerer. So maybe not," Pen cautioned.

"Huh." At least Arisaydia took in the warning without argument. "I admit, I don't like putting myself in a bottle."

"Neither do I," Pen agreed, heartfelt.

"Climb, then."

They did so. It took nearly all their breath, but Arisaydia spared what he could to ask after the numbers and condition of their pursuers, seeming peeved that Pen had no more detailed inventory of their arms.

"You took down, what, seven at the villa? That would leave six for me. It may be better to turn and face them here than letting them catch us later, at a worse vantage, even tireder, in the darkness."

Pen didn't care for Arisaydia's arithmetic. Alone, he thought he might be able to bolt up the hill, turn and dodge, climb, vanish. Run away. *But not the three of us. And so the tactician prevails. In a sense.* He observed, voice flat in his concession, "Velka's Temple-man is going to tie up a lot of my attention, once we get within range of each other. This isn't going to be the kind of fight you think."

Arisaydia's red eyes narrowed. "Can you take him?"

"I...won't know till I see what he brings to the table. We won't exactly be trying to kill each other. Jumping demon problem, there." Among other theological concerns. *Bastard's teeth, what a mess.*

At last Arisaydia stopped, glanced around, and said, "Here. We won't do better."

Pen copied his inspection. The steepest part of the trail zig-zagged down behind them, giving them a height advantage not unlike being atop a rampart. The scrubby slopes to either side allowed no cover for a man to advance and circle them in secret. The defile ahead might not be a good place to be pressed into if anyone did manage to get above them, but it wasn't entirely out of the range of some rabbit-sprint retreat.

Reminding Pen a bit of the prudent sergeant, Arisaydia had them all sit down and share out bites of food from Pen's sack, and mouthfuls of water from the leather bottle he carried, and when had he acquired it? He glanced at Pen's case. "You dragged that all this way?"

"Its contents were expensive, and would be hard to replace. Good steel needles and scissors and scalpels. Clean gauze, the remains of my ointments...

had some trouble getting them compounded correctly, you know."

Nikys eyed it, and him. "I'd have thought you'd be glad to leave it behind."

Yes, no, I don't know, maybe sorry later... "Frugality is a hard habit to break."

Looking thoughtful, Nikys bestirred herself and began gathering up a pile of throwing rocks. Adelis blinked, then went to assist her. Penric wished wanly for his good hunting bow, back in Adria, but joined the foragers.

He stopped when the first of Velka's party, their horses slipping and snorting, cleared the last ridable turn below, looked up, and saw them. Shouts, excitement, bustling back and forth as the ten men and the sergeant dismounted, secured the horses, arrayed themselves and waited. Four of them were archers, Pen saw, even now stringing their short bows and looking up warily, awaiting orders. All their quivers bristled with arrows.

"That's going to be a problem," sighed Arisaydia, watching them.

"Not really," murmured Pen. Nikys glanced at him sidelong and picked up a rock, turning it in her hands. She, too, seemed to be waiting for orders.

"Now I'm sorry you were drawn into our disaster," she said quietly to Pen.

"Wasn't you who did it. And I mean to share that regret around, if I can."

Her little smile reminded him of that scary smirk of her brother's. "Good."

They were just out of bowshot, at least for men shooting uphill. The archers were also out of range for Pen's sorcery, certainly of the finely tuned variety he hoped to use. Landslides remained an option, although there wasn't a great deal of scree poised in just the right places.

More debate below among Velka, the sergeant, and the sorcerer. Then the man in the white robes turned, seemed to steel himself, and began climbing the jagged trail with the aid of a stout staff.

He looked everything a Temple sorcerer and learned divine should be. Tall, grave, mature, powerful, his beard trimmed neatly around his face, though he could have stood to take the scissors to his eyebrows as well; black eyes glared up from their bristling shadows. Both Arisaydia and Nikys stared down in muted alarm.

"This one's my part, I guess," sighed Pen, without enthusiasm. *Des, are we ready?*

Ooh, she cooed, *what a cute little baby demon! What?*

The lad with the beard as well, but his demon is just a youth. Only two animals before him, and this is its first human incarnation. All it will know is what he *knows.*

"Bastard be praised," breathed Pen, and tapped his lips twice with his thumb. Then twice again, because everyone here was going to need His luck to get through the next minutes alive. He stepped out a few paces from where his companions crouched, and let the approaching man get puffed closing their mutual range. He wondered what he looked like in turn. A tired, skinny, sunburned young man with hair escaping its knot—he blew a strand out of his mouth—wearing an odd assortment of cast-offs, sweaty tunic, green jacket, mismatched riding trousers all over horse. Long feet unhappy from his hike in these falling-apart sandals, and he had to get some good boots soon.

"Hedge sorcerer!" the man stopped and shouted up. "I am Learned Kyrato of the Bastard's Order in Patos, and in the god's name I order you to surrender to me. Come peacefully, and no harm will come to you!"

"Demonstrably not the case," Pen shouted back. "Ask Velka what he did to me in the bottle dungeon!"

The man's head went back in perplexity, quickly mastered. "For the second time, I demand your surrender! Or your life will be cast from the Temple's shelter!"

Penric glossed to those at his back, "It's a ritual he's obliged to try. No point in interrupting him before he gets through it."

Kyrato repeated his warning three more times, each more strongly worded. Arisaydia drew his sword and looked even more untrusting. Nikys's dark brows bent in dismayed curiosity.

"I am sorry," said Kyrato solemnly, signed himself, and opened his hand as he attempted to set Pen's clothes and hair on fire.

Pen snapped up the arriving impulse with his cold skill. Kyrato's body jerked slightly, then he tried again, to the same end. And a third time.

It only took that horse two bites to learn better, Des observed, amused.

The sorcerer stared nonplussed at his own hand, then made to ignite Nikys and Arisaydia. Pen whipped those efforts aside even faster, and flipped out the chaos to land where it would; a few rocks worked loose around them and began to tumble downhill. Kyrato dodged, startled. Des was humming like a bowstring released, *Let me, let me, let me...*

"What are you?" Kyrato cried, his eyes widening in real fear at last.

"I *told* Velka I wasn't a hedge sorcerer," Pen returned impatiently. "Didn't he pass you the word? That was really unfair. I swear the man doesn't listen to a thing one says to him."

Pen wondered how inexplicable this intense contest looked to outsiders. Two eccentric men standing on a slope making faces and gesturing at each other...

Velka bellowed up the hill, "Arisaydia! Surrender or be slain!"

Arisaydia muttered, "He meant 'and', there." He gripped his sword in an impatience to match Des's.

The Patos sorcerer put in loudly, "Surrender and your sister will be spared, and be made safe under my authority." Which he probably imagined to be true.

"*Sod* you," snarled Nikys, and heaved her first rock. It was well-aimed, but burst into fragments before it stuck its target. Another followed, to tumble aside in its arc.

"Why don't they hit him?"

Pen wasn't sure if that was plea or complaint. *Both, really.*

Arisaydia dropped a hand on her arm to hold her next launch, muttering, "Useless…"

"No, keep them coming. They're a good distraction." Pen cast her a sunlight smile over his shoulder. "Make him work. Heat him up."

Her eyes flared with understanding. Ha, at least *someone* had listened to him, and remembered. The next rock whistled through the air. Arisaydia woke up and joined her effort, his rocks hissing more viciously.

The sergeant hadn't been an idle spectator. The archers, in two pairs, had edged their way up each side of the slope into tolerable range, and loosed their arrows at last.

Have fun, Des.

The arrows, variously, burst into blue flame as they arced, to arrive on target as harmless puffs of ash, or tumbled end-over-end to clatter on the stones. A second flight met the same fate.

Why doesn't he move faster? Doesn't he have the trick of it? asked Pen, his senses racing along with Des's.

He's controlling his demon tightly. They can only do one thing at a time. It's almost sad, really.

Remember, he's a fellow divine, not your plaything.

Then he shouldn't have threatened you.

The archers had almost worked close enough for Pen to reach, but as long as they were content to waste arrows, Pen was content to let them. A little closer, and he could clip their bowstrings at will, and their hamstrings nearly as easily. Pen trusted Kyrato had more defenses than thus seen, but since Pen hadn't really attacked him yet, he'd had nothing to demonstrate them upon. Pen was growing adroit with that brutal tweak to the sciatic nerves, if he wanted to render this enemy unable to run away, not really his preference here. But the axilla offered equally distracting possibilities...

The sorcerer shifted the dusty pebbles under Pen's feet, trying to dump him on his backside presumably; Pen danced aside to solider stone. A formless flurry of hallucinations whirled before Pen's eyes; an interesting natural talent, suggesting the man could create extraordinary visions someday, with practice. Though not today, alas. Even without Des's aid, Pen had no trouble ignoring them. The sorcerer was momentarily distracted averting one of Arisaydia's sizzling projectiles—during which Nikys's latest lob came down square on his head with a satisfying *thunk*. That had been a heavy rock she'd heaved, two-handed. He fell half-stunned, sliding down the path and grabbing at his staff to stop himself. With a distraught cry, he flung out his hands.

Pain boomed in Pen's chest as his heart tried to tear itself apart. He went over backwards as if hit by a ram. Des was abruptly nowhere else but inside him, wrapping herself around the organ, holding it back together. The next flight of arrows fell unimpeded all around them, missing by inches.

Yells from below as the soldiers, taking his fall as their signal, started forward.

Pen climbed to his knees, chest bucking for air, mouth gaping in astonishment. That had been a *killing blow.*

Kyrato was also on his knees, mouth open in dismay and horrified triumph. He hadn't quite, Pen thought, intended to do that forbidden thing, but he didn't look as though he wanted to call it back. His gaze jerked all around, as he struggled to guess where Penric's demon would jump as he drew his last breath.

Chaos *spewed* from Desdemona.

Half the hillside shook itself apart and thundered downward.

Kyrato slithered several yards with it, ending half-buried in scree. Sweating and scarlet, he heaved, twisted, drained suddenly pale, and then... passed out.

Heat stroke, Pen diagnosed, from some strange detached plane of continued consciousness, as uncomfortable and unwelcome as his trip to the bottle dungeon. His chest *ached*. The rest of him wasn't doing terribly well, either, although there was a nice moment when frantic hands gathered him into a soft, soft lap.

Arisaydia's boots passed him by; a sudden scrape and clang of steel rang descant over the throbbing echo of the slide.

"Don't kill the sorcerer!" Pen cried in warning.

A grunt, a scuffle. "I remember," Arisaydia's voice floated back, sounding irritated. "Didn't he?"

"Oh Mother's blood, Pen, are you all right?" Nikys choked above him. Wet drops splashed his face, although the early evening sky was an impossible deep blue, cloudless. Could tears be also a blessing? But gods, he loved the sky in this country.

"Will be." *I hope.* "Don't you need to keep throwing rocks right now?"

"You just threw all of them. I think Adelis has it under control...the rest are running away. I mean, the ones who can. The sergeant is yelling for them to come back, but he's running just as hard."

"Huh. Good." *Des...?*

...Des...?

Hsh. B'sy. But then, after a moment, in muzzy indignation: *Kyrato was going to* sacrifice *his* demon, *in killing you. Let the god take it with your soul.* He *would have lived.*

Aye. War-rules magic. S'why I want nothing to do with war.

...Good.

XVI

NIKYS CLUTCHED PENRIC, whose mumbling had drifted into well-enunciated but not particularly sensible rambling, and watched Adelis's figure move methodically around the slope below. The sun had retreated behind the hills, leaving the sky still luminous, only a few stars pricking through, and the dry ground drenched in shadowless blue. Adelis had chased off the only two swordsmen still willing to stand up and try to fight after the landslide. Both of them cut and bleeding, their considerable courage had broken, and they'd turned to run down the trail after their fleeing comrades while they still could. Nikys was relieved.

Adelis paused at an indistinct shape at the bottom of the slide. Muffled voices, a cry of protest, a meaty *thunk*. Silence. Nikys shuddered, inhaled, looked away.

Penric convulsed up in her lap. "What was that? He's not dispatching all the wounded, is he? I have to stop him—"

"No. Or only one, I think. Lie still. How badly are you hurt?"

He sank back. "Not too badly, I think." His inner twin's voice overrode this, puffing, oddly, more: "Nearly killed just now. Would have been, except for me."

"Des!" objected Pen, and shut his jaw on this.

What did it say that Nikys had better luck getting a straight answer from a chaos demon than a man? *Nothing new, more's the pity.* "Desdemona, what's really going on? Tell me!"

Penric clenched his teeth, but then gave up, or gave way. "That accursed Bastard's divine tried to rip apart his heart, by forbidden magic. I have it under control for now, but Penric should stay flat in bed for the next week."

Nikys stared around the dusky hills at the marked absence of beds, and sighed. "Was that... normal magic?"

"No," said Desdemona, and Penric, one hand wavering up to touch her face, added, "No one should be allowed to break my heart but you, Madame Owl."

Her breath caught, but before they could continue this promising exchange, Adelis came clumping back. He paused below to study the unconscious sorcerer half-buried in the scree, then bent to wipe his sword clean on the loose sleeve of the man's white robe, and sheathed it. Mounting the hill to Nikys's side, he let down a pair of bows and a quiver of arrows. With a tired grunt, he dropped next to them and gazed out over the unexpected battlefield.

Penric levered up on his elbow. "What all has happened? Is happening...?"

"The sergeant, two archers, and two men ran off, for now. And the two wounded, after. The rest are half-buried in the rubble. A few may get out without help, and help the others. I expect their comrades will come creeping back to their aid by-and-by. The horses tore loose and ran off during what I take to be your landslide. At least one fell. Broken neck, fortunately. Broken legs would have made for a messier cleanup. For somebody, not for us. We need to move along."

Penric's brows pinched. "What about Velka?"

Adelis shrugged. "He'd tried for me twice. Three times, if what you say is true. I decided not to give him a fourth chance."

"Oh." Penric sank back, signing himself. "I regret...not doing better with him."

"Well, he's his god's problem now. Don't promote your troubles beyond your rank."

"That is actually theologically sound advice."

"Works in the army, too."

"Ah." Penric hesitated. "Did you ever find out his real name?"

"Didn't ask. Didn't care, by then."

"It seems strange to kill a man without even knowing his name."

"Seems usual to me." Adelis rolled his shoulders. "Though in his case, we may find out later. Anyway, with the head cut off, the body will thrash. Best guess it will take this lot some days to dig themselves out and limp back for help. More confusion after that. Unless that one"—he nodded downhill to the pale lump that was the Patos sorcerer—"recovers faster than I think. Which, given his demon, your god only knows."

Penric, who had slumped into Nikys's willing lap, struggled up again. "I should try to treat the wounded—"

"No, you shouldn't," said Nikys, pushing him back.

"No, and I won't help," Desdemona put in. "I have other priorities right now. They'll all live if their friends return."

"I agree with the demon," said Adelis, unexpectedly both for the agreement, and for spotting just who had spoken the words coming out of Penric's mouth. "I swear the thing has more sense than you do, Learned Fool."

Which was, all right, a small step toward acknowledging the truth of Penric's account of himself. An Adelis-inch. Nikys bent her face and smiled.

"Any being learns a lot in two hundred years," Penric conceded shakily.

Adelis picked up one bow and tested it. "You said you could shoot flaming arrows, sorcerer. How about regular ones?"

"Usually. Maybe not right now."

He handed the bow to Nikys. "Check the draw for you."

Seated on the ground, she took it a little awkwardly, twisted and pulled, and grimaced. "It's fairly hard for me, but I could do it in a pinch." She leaned over and set it with the other.

"We'll keep both, then." Adelis turned and shifted his gaze upward. "I'm not sure how much steep we have left, but if we can get through that narrow place before full dark, we should be able to stop safely till moonrise."

Nikys bit her lip, wondering how this squared with Desdemona's recommendation of rest for Penric's safe recovery. It did not sound good.

The pile of pale cloth below them shifted, then moaned.

This time, Penric rose in greater determination. "Help me. I have to get some water down that one, or he won't last till morning. It matters, trust me."

"Jumping demon problem?" inquired Adelis, in a kind of wearied concession.

"At the very least. Not that he deserves to keep his."

Nikys hoisted the leather bottle, and Penric. They slid down the few yards and settled by the half-buried sorcerer.

Penric took the bottle and dribbled water over the man's head, rubbing it into his hair. "I need to cool him down the hard way, if he's still too stunned to shed chaos," Penric told her. "Here, Learned Kyrato." He patted the man's bearded cheek. "Wake up, now. You have to drink this." He tilted the spout to the man's lips.

Kyrato swallowed, choked, spilled, and seemed to come back to full consciousness. He heaved his trapped body, without effect.

"Stop struggling," Penric told him, a stern hand to his shoulder. "You'll just make yourself hotter. I haven't much time—"

Kyrato's voice went sharp in terror. "I won't tell you anything!"

"Good, because I only want you to listen," said Penric.

"Is this safe?" asked Nikys in worry. "If he just tried to kill you?"

"Now that I'm on my guard, yes. ...Maybe. You'd best sit back a way." Penric gestured.

Nikys retreated perhaps two feet, and felt around for a good big piece of scree, ready to knock Kyrato in the head with it again if he made some sudden move. Although it wasn't the moves she could see but the ones she couldn't that were the real danger, she supposed. She'd have to trust in Penric and Desdemona for those. This was... curiously not-hard.

Kyrato's eyes flickered from her back to Penric.

"The fight's over," Penric informed him. "Your side lost. You have surrendered."

Groggily, Kyrato said, "No, I haven't." He mustered resolve. "You may get away this time, but the Bastard's Order will track you down."

"Which will be ridiculously easy, as I work for the Bastard's Order. And the white god."

Kyrato managed a shaky sneer. "Who are you to speak for the white god? Have you met Him?"

"Once, about eleven years ago. Not an experience a man forgets." He shrugged. "Nor does a demon. You can call me Learned...Anonymous for now, although if we ever meet again in less troubled circumstances I promise I'll introduce myself properly."

Kyrato looked as though he didn't believe a word of this. No—as though not-believing was less *frightening* than believing. Most curious. Nikys watched with increasing fascination.

"I have not much time," Penric went on, "but I need to speak to you about the way you are treating your demon. Because it's both theologically incorrect—and rude and cruel," someone added aside, "and very poor management, frankly.

"Your demon is a gift of the god and the Temple, you know, an elegant opportunity for mutual growth, not a beast to be dominated, imprisoned, and enslaved. To it, you are model, mentor, and the only parent such an elemental being can have. As the holder of a Temple demon, you have an obligation to pass it on at the end of your life improved, not ruined by your selfishness, inattention, or, as in this case, fear, bad judgment, and panic." Penric waved a hand. "Although I grant you were led astray."

Learned Kyrato's stare of terror was slowly transmuting to a stare of utter disbelief. *Oh good*, thought Nikys, *it's not just me.* Even the Temple-trained found Penric confusing.

"I don't know if or how you will be able to make things right with your demon," Penric went on, "although I would certainly suggest repentance, prayer, and meditation for a start. Forgiveness will likely be beyond it until it is not beyond you, and as for absolution, you'll need to petition a higher authority. But I would suggest, by way of a first apology, and also a good idea for your future association, that you start by gifting it with a nice name." Penric sat up and smiled cheerfully at the trapped divine. Kyrato responded by heaving again against his stony prison, to no effect. No—heaving away from Penric.

"You are mad," choked Kyrato.

"My brother says he's as mad as three boots," Nikys put in from the side, agreeably, starting to get into the spirit of this. "But he's also a very learned divine, with a very wise demon. You should attend."

In a hoarse voice, Kyrato said, "It is ascendant!" Then a rather cross-eyed look. "No...but it is monstrous dense. I thought it must be ascendant." His voice rose sharp again. "*Why isn't it ascendant?*"

"That's just what I'm trying to explain," said Penric patiently. "Now, names. Can you think of one you'd like?" He looked hopefully at Kyrato, who was starting to wheeze. Penric frowned and forced him to swallow another drink of water.

Abandoning the divine, Penric turned his expression inward. "Des, do you have any ideas for naming a young fellow demon?" A pause. "That's absurd." Another pause. "And that's obscene." And another, "No, we're not naming it after me, either." He sighed and turned to Nikys. "Madame Khatai? What's a Cedonian name that you like?"

Nikys, in your mouth, she thought, but offered aloud, "Reseen? Kuna? Sarande?"

"Des," said Penric, "does Learned Kyrato's demon have a preference? No?" He frowned again at Kyrato. "Really, how long have you possessed the poor thing that it doesn't understand the simplest of nomenclatures?"

He appeared to think, although not very long, then sat up. "All right." Penric signed himself and placed his hand on Kyrato's brow, following to do so again as the man recoiled. "In the white god's name I bless you and name you Kuna. A somewhat catch-as-catch-can name-giving ceremony," he added aside to Nikys, "but you and Des are two adults and can bear witness, so it's sufficiently sanctified."

As Kyrato was no longer struggling to escape, or much of anything apart from lying there limply in a state of receding heat stroke and advancing Penric, Nikys retreated uphill while Penric continued sermonizing. Adelis had finished organizing their belongings.

"Does he ever shut up?" Adelis inquired in mild gloom.

"I think he talks more when he's tired. Makes less sense then, though." She collected the few undamaged arrows that had fallen in their vicinity, adding them to the quiver.

Penric finished his lecture at last, signed the distraught man, tapped his own lips twice with his thumb, and climbed—well, crawled—back up to them, where he lay on his back and tried to catch his breath. Adelis studied the too-rapid rise and fall of his chest, and shook his head ruefully. "Aye. I see the problem."

"Shall we each take an arm?" asked Nikys.

"Better, I think, if you take the food, water, bows, and...yes, my sword."

"And his case?"

"If you choose. I'll lug the blond fool for you. Consider it your belated Bastard's Day present, sister."

"Ah, yes, you missed the last one, didn't you?"

"Busy with a war at the time, which I'm sure your god would understand. I almost dedicated it to Him."

Penric argued, but he was outvoted three to one, and at last he was coaxed up onto Adelis's back. Adelis's legs bent a little, then straightened. "Heavier than he looks," he grunted.

"I'm sure I could make it on my own—" Penric began, to which Nikys and Adelis replied in unison, "Shut up, Penric." Nikys thought Desdemona would have chimed in to the chorus if she could.

In the defile, the shadows were growing purple. This stretch, rough underfoot, was a hard slog by any standard. Nikys and Adelis saved their breaths, although Penric was still talking, going on about something in Wealdean until Adelis threatened to drop him back down the hill. His head drooped to Adelis's shoulder, and then there were only the deepening twilight sounds of the hills: small insects, a nightingale calling, the crunch of the dirt and gravel below their feet, and then the faintest flutter of a bat. As they came up out of the winding rift, an owl swooped by not ten feet overhead, wings spread in vast silence, and Nikys could see the white glint of Penric's teeth as he looked up and smiled.

A question occurred to her. Happily, she had just the person to answer it right here. "Desdemona," she said, "if Penric had been killed"—horrid thought—"and you had been forced to jump, where would you have gone? If the demon always chooses the strongest person in the vicinity, it would have had to be Adelis, right?"

Adelis jerked, then paused to heave his slipping passenger back up and labor on. It was too dark to see his expression, but Nikys imagined it a study in dismay.

"No, child," said Desdemona. "It would have been you."

At this, Adelis stopped short. Nikys stopped with him. "Me! Why me?"

"We have been with Penric for eleven years, and are now well imprinted with him. We could have made no other choice."

Penric breathed out, and Nikys could see the faint sapphire gleam of his widening eyes, but for once he was struck silent. After a moment, they hiked on.

No sounds of pursuit arose behind them.

A prayer of supplication to the Bastard was begging for trouble, in many people's views, but Nikys thought a prayer of gratitude for His better gifts was not likely to go wrong. She hummed the old hymn of praise under her breath as they reached a flatter trail. "Sing it aloud," entreated Penric from his perch. "I've never heard it in Cedonian."

She looked up to find no up left; before them, now, the land fell away in velvety darkness. A hundred miles distant it rose again, like a black blanket rucked up upon the horizon, the promise of Orbas.

"Far enough," huffed Adelis, and let down his burden. They all found seats upon the stony ground, under the sweep of the stars. She shared the water pouch around.

Then Nikys straightened and took up the old words, as Penric had requested. Adelis came in on the chorus in a bass harmony, as he had not done since they'd sung in the temple as youths, before... everything. Penric murmured in a pleased way, and then, at Nikys's demand, offered up a hymn of his own in his native Wealdean, in a breathy but surprisingly true baritone.

His words fell strange and sweet upon her ears, and so, trading mysteries, they sang up the moonrise.